There's only one Mann,
TIGER MANN—
America's tough, sexy, deadly
new espionage agent—who is
always ready to play the
relentless,
kill-or-be-killed
game of international intrigue
. . . even on the day of his own
wedding.

———————————

"A gala one for mystery fans. . . . Tiger slugs,
shoots and loves through international intrigue
at a fast pace."
—*Charlotte Observer*

"Tiger Mann wins through again."
—*Saturday Review Syndicate*

"What a piece of work is Tiger Mann."
—*Springfield Sun*

Mickey Spillane

BLOODY SUNRISE

A SIGNET BOOK
published by
The New American Library

SIGNET TRADEMARK REG. U.S. PAT. OFF. AND FOREIGN COUNTRIES
REGISTERED TRADEMARK—MARCA REGISTRADA
HECHO EN CHICAGO, U.S.A.

SIGNET BOOKS are published by
The New American Library, Inc.
1301 Avenue of the Americas, New York, New York 10019

PRINTED IN THE UNITED STATES OF AMERICA

To: Nat Drutman and the days of
the Kaydets and the AAF when
the blue yonder was really
wild and even wilder when you
got shot out of it.

It was Saturday and I was going to be married. But it **1**
was dawn and too early, yet I couldn't sleep thinking
of what was going to happen later and that twenty
blocks farther uptown Rondine would be curled up in a bed,
naked and inviting, still asleep, and in a little while there
never would be a city mile between us again.

Mentally I had already composed the letter of resignation
Martin Grady would get. He wouldn't like it. He'd do his
damndest to stop it but his damndest wouldn't be good
enough. The day of the guns was past. The Soviets could take
me off their "A" list and any future targets Grady had planned
for me could breathe a little easier because whoever came at
them wouldn't be quite as good, nor as fast or even enjoy the
work as much as I had. The odds for them would be better,
even if not good enough, and they'd fall like all the others.
But at least they'd die knowing they did have a better chance
of survival.

I wondered what Grady would say. Appeal to my
patriotism? Maybe he'd remind me that nobody ever came off
the "A" list. I'd always be a Red target if for nothing better
than to teach the rest of them a lesson. When one of us went
down all of us felt the impact. Or would he use the old dodge
about me, like the others, having some psychological quirk
that made staying in the business a necessity in order to
satisfy our compulsions? Grady could be mighty persuasive,
but one thought of Rondine could make a far more formidable
argument for my side.

Grady boy, I'm cutting out. No more guns, no more kills.
I'm walking out of the jungle alive and staying that way. I

liked the dough and the work fine, but now I love something more. Tiger Mann has been on his last hunt and now the name changes, the locale differs and the future opens. I bury the .45 in a closet for a keepsake and go into the vine-covered-cottage routine. I've seen the world and helped change it. I met the people and helped kill some. I don't like what I've done. So now I'll change Tiger Mann. Sorry, buddy, but that's how it goes. That's how Rondine wants it. That's how I want it, too.

The phone beside me let out a sharp, discordant note and I reached for it, annoyed. It was still a little before seven and I hadn't put any calls in. As soon as I lifted the receiver a voice said, "Tiger?"

"Yeah."

"Wally Gibbons." His voice sounded tired.

"What're you doing up this early? You Broadway columnists never . . ."

"I haven't been to bed yet."

"So why roust me out?"

"Because I got a call from a guy who says he knows you. He read about the last business in my column and contacted me to find you. Now I didn't tell him a damn thing. I said I'd see if I could find you and pass on the message."

"A lot of people would like to find me," I said.

"That's why I didn't say anything. You know a guy named Clement Fletcher?"

I ran through a list of names in my head and couldn't place it. "Describe him."

"I can't. It was a phone call. He rang my office eight times before I got the call, and he said it was urgent I get hold of you. Anyway, he left a number. Call it if you want to." He reeled it off and I jotted it down absently.

"What did he say, Wally?"

"Nothing. He wouldn't talk. He was excited about something and one of those guys who chew up a mouthpiece. Talked in a whisper, made it fast and said that somehow I should get you to call. Know what it's about?"

I put the pencil down and stretched out on the bed. "Not the slightest, buddy. I don't give a damn either. I'll make the call but if it's got anything to do with my job I'll toss it in the hopper and let somebody else pick it up. I'm getting married today."

"So I heard. Good luck. You'll need it."

"Thanks, but why?"

"To stay that way. Or maybe just to stay alive. Ever since I found out about you I don't even want to be on the same side of the street where you are."

"Drop dead." I laughed at him and hung up. This was one day nobody was going to spoil for me.

The sun was cutting across the top of the skyline and reaching in the window with waxy yellow rays. Twenty stories down the city was coming to life with the birth pangs of noise only the garbage collectors can make, the shrill screech of metal on pavement as loud as the chain loaders on the trucks. Farther off a siren moaned its sympathy and dwindled to silence behind the walls of Broadway, and dot by dot, the specks of people began their endless thread toward the great holes on the street that led underground to the veins and arteries of New York that would circulate them to some other wound in some other street where they would work or play.

Me, I was going to get married and dump the whole bit.

Clement Fletcher.

There was something familiar about it but I couldn't remember where or when. Or who.

It wasn't a big name. It had to be pretty far down the line because in my business you couldn't afford to forget important names, or even unimportant ones. This was just a name, yet somehow familiar.

Friend? I didn't have that many.

And enemies don't call first. They just kill.

The call couldn't have come through Martin Grady or any of the organization because there would have been a signal word involved, giving the degree of urgency or related to a target, so it had to be personal. But I was still on the Soviet's "A" list and there was no telling how they worked. They could set up some pretty cute traps at times.

Whoever said curiosity killed the cat said a mouthful. If it had just been another name I would have forgotten about it, but this one came from the past and had enough of a familiar touch so that I couldn't leave it alone.

I called Wally Gibbons back, got him out of the sack, swearing up a storm, and asked him to get a reverse on the number so I'd have an address to go with it, dropped the phone back, waited ten minutes and he came up with a West Side residence a block off the river and an invitation for me to drop dead, too.

A quick shower and shave took the sleep out of me and I pulled on my clothes. Out of force of habit I fitted the shoulder holster on, snapped it on my belt, then remembered what day it was. I grinned, said the hell with it and almost took it off. The .45 was an old job, but there were times when it had been my best friend. It was going to be hard to discard it.

So okay, old friend, just one more time.

I shoved it into the black leather sling, tried the spring clip to make sure it threw out properly, then went downstairs, had a cup of coffee at the breakfast counter and grabbed a cab at the front door. It was too early for heavy traffic, so I was able to make sure nobody was on my tail then settled back until we got over to the row of antiquated brownstones that ran perpendicular to the river and the wharves that bordered it.

The number was the third in from the bridging that was the West Side Highway, a dilapidated rooming house with a crumbling sandstone stoop and a dirty front that advertised with an enameled metal plaque on the door. Just one word. ROOMS.

I rang the bell twice before a tiny old lady came to the door, wiping her mouth on her apron, two rolls of toilet paper clutched under one arm.

"You looking for a place, son?"

I winked at her. "A friend. Clement Fletcher. Think it's too early to get him up?"

Her eyes went up and down me slowly, then her face wrinkled in a smile. "Didn't think he had such friends, but you can't tell anymore. Had a boy in here last week said Judge Long was his father, and he was. The judge even came here. Gave him hell for shipping out, but the boy left again yesterday. Went out on the *Maitland,* same one my mister used to work. He was an A.B., he was. Good, too. You'll find Mr. Fletcher next floor, up front."

"I'll find him. Thanks."

I went up the stairs, heard the landlady shut a door on the floor below and unloaded the .45, cocking the hammer back under my thumb. There was only one door to Fletcher's room and I stood beside it, listening. From inside came the gentle rumble of a snore. The second pick I used on the lock opened it and I eased the door open, stepped inside and closed it behind me.

The guy was sleeping in a chair, yesterday's *News* lying across his lap, his head buried against one wing of the mohair monstrosity that was the third piece of furniture in the place. He was somewhere in his middle fifties, a small guy in dungarees and unbuttoned shirt with a fresh haircut and not-so-fresh shave. His mouth was open and he breathed heavily, evenly, each snore a soft burble of unconscious contentment. On the dresser beside the bed was a handful of bills and the top two were C-notes, the rest all fifties.

I stood in front of him, knowing that I had seen him before, yet still unable to recollect where it was. When I was satisfied that he was clean, I nudged his foot with mine, took a step back with the .45 leveled at his gut and watched him come awake.

All he said when he saw me was, "Goddamn, Tiger! I . . ." Then he saw the rod in my fist and closed his mouth hard, swallowed and looked at me.

"Where do I know you from, Fletcher?"

"Geez, Tiger, I . . ."

"Fast, buddy. No long talks. Where?"

He let go the arms of the chair, his eyes fascinated by the sight of the .45. Finally he nodded, found the words and said, "Like Panama, man! Remember?"

"No."

He thumped his finger against his chest. "You dragged me out of the bay. Damn, I was drowning. You hauled my ass on the dock and ran them thieving bastards off who grabbed my roll and saved my life!"

Then I remembered him and put the rod back under my coat. A crazy seaman who saved his dough instead of blowing it, setting himself up for a pack of gooks who saw him flash it. They had rolled him when he was drunk and dumped him when I was on the dock trying to find where Messner had planted the explosives and I was in time to punch a few holes in the natives, grab his kick back and get him out of the drink.

So now I had an everlasting friend who wanted to buy me a drink. I grinned at him, stuck out my hand and he took it with a grin that went all the way across his face. "Sorry I forgot, Fletch." I tapped my side where the .45 hung. "I'm in a business where you can't take chances."

"Yeah, I know, Tiger. Damn, you gimme a scare. I don't like all that iron pointed at me."

"Gibbons passed on your call to me. Now look, I'd like to bust a few with you for old time's sake, but I'm getting married today and I have to stay clean. Good to see you and if we meet up again maybe we can have a few, but I have to scratch off."

"Hell, Tiger, I didn't call you for that." His face screwed up into a frown and he squirmed out of the chair. He looked at me, walked to the window and parted the curtains for a glance at the street, then turned around. "I read about you."

"So did a lot of people."

"I remembered the name."

I nodded.

"After Panama word got around the ship and I knew who it was broke the trouble. I didn't say nothing, Tiger. I never told nobody about you being on the docks and all that."

"Thanks."

He waved his hand and grimaced. "It ain't that why I called you. Like I said, I knew about you from what was said and because we was on top of it all. I figured you was somebody special after they hushed up that deal when the warehouse blew and those guys was killed. I knowed it was you, all right. I heard that fink punk Billy Mendes describe you, but I didn't say nothing. Okay?"

"Okay."

I knew there had been a watcher that night, but I never knew who it was. I had seen the movement from behind the bales and didn't have to clean up the action. Friend Fletcher never knew how close to dying he had been. Billy Mendes had died before he could sign a statement or make an identification positive.

"Then why did you call me, Fletch?"

He wiped his hand across his face, chipped at his teeth with a thumbnail, then plunked down on the edge of the bed. Very quietly he said, "So I don't know who else to call. I buzz the fuzz and they laugh, I go it alone and I get trouble. Hell, I don't know what to do until I read about you."

"What kind of trouble?" I asked him.

He eased his eyes up to me. "You'll laugh."

"Why?"

"Because it don't sound for real."

"Tell me anyway."

Clement Fletcher had something big on his mind. To him, anyway. He sat there a minute trying to think out what he had to say, then: "Remember the roll you got me back?"

"Uh-huh."

"So I saved up another grand. I worked for it, too. In Brussels I found this guy."

"What guy?" I asked him.

"Like I told you, Tiger, I want to go to Perdes outside of Vera Cruz where they got uranium. I always did want to go there. Wells and Chobeay told me about them strikes in U there and I wanted to go. You think I want to sail all my life? You think I want to hustle ..."

"Get to the point?"

He looked at me from between his fingers. "So in Brussels I buy a Geiger counter."

"How much?"

"Eighteen hundred bucks. I blew my roll."

"You got robbed too. They're on the market for two-fifty here."

He jumped out of the chair and went back to the window. "So I got robbed. I don't know. They said I needed it for going to Perdes. I play with it on the ship. I can tell hot watches from cool ones."

"That's no test."

"Screw you."

I knew he had a sore spot and felt sorry for the words. "Okay, Fletch, so what's the bit? I got to go. I don't come running for just anybody and this is a big day for me."

"Geez, Tiger, I'm sorry."

"Forget it."

He nodded, banged his hands together and finally stopped his pacing long enough to face me. "I come in on the *Maitland,* y' know?"

"I know."

"In Germany they load three presses. I'm down in the hold with the counter and it starts to run off. Going like hell. I track it down and I pick up a crate ... big one ... them damn presses are big. One's hot."

"Go on."

"I check it out ... I mark the crate. It's hot. It's got uranium in it."

"A crateful?"

"I didn't look."

He didn't want to look at me at all. He kept staring out the window wondering what I'd say, and he was feeling like a jerk and I couldn't blame him. I said, "Let's take a look at it."

And it was my good deed for the day. I could wind up my operation with a favor to a friend who had been took and maybe ease his misery when he found out the answer ... then I could get married and cut out.

It took a call and a promise to get where we wanted to go, but we got inside the warehouse and found the crate that Fletcher had marked off and it didn't take too long to get inside it. About thirty more cases were around the big one, packed with accessories, but this was the one he had marked off.

The German firm of Keipleitz was one of the foremost manufacturers of rotary presses in the world and to make one took almost a year, but because the press could turn out some fantastic runs, the firm had the biggest demand from every publishing house in the world. Luckily, we were their biggest buyers. This one was consigned to somewhere in Washington, D.C.

After the fourth board we climbed inside and there it was.

A rotary press.

Complete, excepting accessories.

Not one thing that shouldn't be there, and when we got out and put the boards back I looked at Clement Fletcher and said, "No gimmick, Fletch."

"I'm telling you, that counter . . ."

"Fletch . . . I know printing from old Kelly's to the newest rotaries. I went over that job. There's no gimmick."

"Tiger . . . the counter . . ."

"Suppose we look at the counter."

"Why?"

"Let's look at it, okay?"

"Sure, Tiger. It's on the ship."

But it wasn't. He searched all over his section of the hold and came up with only the empty box in his hands and a blank look on his face and I knew what had happened.

I said, "Fletcher . . ."

"Look, Tiger . . ."

I stopped him. "Buddy, you got a salted gimmick. For eighteen hundred bucks they hand you a simple frame you couldn't tell from a Geiger counter or a radarscope that clicks at certain times and you got stuck. Face it, you lost your loot and to make sure there were no kickbacks, the sellers hired somebody on board to dump it for a fin and you are out, Fletch, O—U—T. Did you see the timer on that press?"

"No."

"It had a luminous dial. A big one. It could start any Geiger-type reactor working like hell. You zeroed in on that. You got stuck, friend."

He got it all at once. All he could say was, "Oh, hell," then we walked outside, went back where we came from and found a diner where we had a cup of coffee together.

It was a year-old reunion and for a while we were able to

talk about the broads back in Panama and what had happened there, but his heart wasn't in it at all. In front of his eyes he could see the eighteen hundred bucks doing him out of an expedition to Perdes, and even though he lost it I couldn't tell him how lucky he was. The big con was worse than the little con.

At noon I shook hands with him and walked up three long blocks before I found a cab and got a ride back to the hotel.

For a guy's wedding day it had really started off with a squash, but maybe I was just as lucky. At four I'd be married and that would be the end of it.

I went upstairs and started getting my things together. One leather bag took everything I carried and the rest was in my pocket. I snapped the bag shut, picked up the phone to call for a bellboy so I could go down in style one last time and before I could speak the desk clerk said, "There's a call for you, sir, will you take it?"

I thought it would be Rondine. I said, "Please," too fast.

And Martin Grady said, "Tiger, you're on assignment. *Plato.*"

Plato was the big one. Kill or be killed. The entire structure of America was in trouble. The alternate answer was war.

She opened the door when I knocked and stood there **2** tall and beautiful, the green belted housecoat nipping in her waist and accentuating the flare of her hips, the neckline rolled open so that the velvet swell of her breasts was barely visible and dipped into the smooth contour of her stomach. Behind her the sunlight put streaks of gold through her auburn hair, and her lips parted in a smile of pure love.

I said, "Hello, Rondine."

But she wasn't Rondine. She was Edith Caine and Rondine was a long time dead, her elder sister who looked exactly like her twenty years ago. The war years, I thought, wild, incredible years that seem almost unreal now. The first Rondine had twisted her thinking until she walked out of the Caine household and into the Nazi camp as an espionage agent to fight her own kind. And I was the OSS agent who had tracked her down in occupied France to kill her ... and wound up in love instead. That was ... until she put two slugs in me to save her own hide and left me to die. I carried a big hate inside me after that. I carried a picture of that beautiful face and body I could never forget, then I saw it again long after she was really dead ... but this time the component belonged to Edith, her younger sister. To me, though, Edith would always be Rondine whom I had loved and she didn't mind because I loved *her* even more. I had almost killed her because I thought she was Rondine. Now? Now I'd kill for her or because of her as she would for me.

"Tiger." She held out her hand and I took it. Her mouth was a soft passionate flower on mine, hot, wet ... her fingers biting into my arms as I pulled her to me so that we seemed to melt into one huge explosive emotion.

Still, there was something wrong and she felt it. She took her mouth from mine, pushed back in the cradle of my arms and looked at me with quizzical eyes. "Darling . . . what is it?" Her voice had a low husky note.

"Let's sit down."

She hooked her arm under mine and we went inside. It wasn't going to be easy, this. I let her bring me coffee first, drank half of it while she waited patiently, then I said, "We have to hold the wedding, doll."

The hurt that flashed into her eyes was a quick thing. It came and went, leaving a gentle, sad look that had too much understanding in it. "Can you tell me?"

I shook my head. "No. I'm sorry."

"But today . . ."

"I was going to wire in a resignation. This came up before I could. It's too big to drop and there isn't anyone else who can handle it."

"No one?"

"Kitten . . . it involves the total security of this country and possibly yours, too. Britain and the U.S. are tied in so tight that what affects one affects the other. I can't back out of it. I gave you a half-ass explanation of my work and that's as far as I can go. We have a code and a set of rules we can't abrogate and won't, not for anything. I'm sorry as hell, baby, but even before you comes this and I hope you can understand."

"It . . . isn't easy." She looked away suddenly, her mouth set in a forced smile. "I really don't know what to say."

"There isn't anything to say. Let me do it and get it over with. Then I'll be back."

Her eyes found mine again and they were curiously round. "Will you?"

"I've always made it before."

"Will this be . . . like the last time? With me?" She put her coffee cup down and folded her hands in her lap. "How many men did you kill then, Tiger? How many times did they try to kill you? The odds may be in your favor but the law of averages isn't anymore."

"Rondine . . ."

"No, Tiger, let me tell you. Before there was a coldness about you. It worked to your advantage. You aren't the same anymore and now you can lose. You may not come back this time and all the while I'll be waiting. It isn't easy to live with."

I got up and fiddled with my hat. "When it's over I'll be back."

"I may not be here."

"I'll find you."

"I don't mean that. I've lived with too many things too long. I thought I had found the love and security I had always dreamed about and when that's put in jeopardy I'll be all empty inside and there could be somebody else. There almost was . . . once."

There wasn't much I could say. I couldn't explain and I couldn't argue and I wasn't about to do either. There never was a broad in the world that couldn't wait if she wanted to and if she didn't, well . . .

I said, "The wheel's already turning, kid. Pick your number or not. But I'll be back. Some things just don't change. I'm one." I walked to the door, looked back at her once and winked. Her face never changed its sad smile and I knew how she felt inside. It had happened to me once before too.

One hell of a way to begin a wedding day was all I could think. One hell of a way.

I got my luggage out of the Chester, down into a cab and checked into the King Leopold under the cover name of H. Talbot according to Grady's instructions. I waited a half hour and called the Newark Control, asked for Virgil Adams and got him, gave the prearranged signal and said, "Tiger Mann, here. It's *Plato* and the number is four-four-nine-one. Are we identified?"

"Cross-check. Templeton two."

"Dartmouth," I said.

"Roger, Tiger. I knew your voice anyway. The BX tapped your freq but we had to be sure."

"Two-twenty-one from Stitch. I need all the information. They got me in cold on this one."

"That's what Grady said. You know about the defector Gabin Martrel?"

"I read about it."

"Okay, they got him here. He's in the Church Street office of IATS and has a blanket around him."

"Why?"

"This guy was head of OONA-3 and is possibly one of the most important links in the interspy bit. He was a single exchange and his record is wild. He was part of their ballistics missile security, ran the Beltov Project and is loaded with names and places that could put us on top."

"Why?"

"What else could make a guy switch teams?"

"Decency, integrity," I said. "That's two reasons."

"Give me another."

"A dame."

"You hit it, brother rat. Now process it."

"My pleasure," I told him and slammed the phone back. It was the story of my life all over again. One goddamn dame and you're dead. Or alive. But either way it's trouble.

Wally Gibbons picked me up at seven in the Blue Ribbon Restaurant on Forty-fourth Street with Dave Severn, the political legman for his paper, in tow. By then I had read and clipped all the items from the major dailies and had them laid out on the table. Every one of them was an official news release and none of the reporters seemed to have an inside track, so I was hoping Severn could come up with something.

So far, all that was said was that Gabin Martrel, a top man in Soviet operations, had asked for political asylum the first day he had arrived in this country with the Soviet delegation that was here to begin disarmament talks.

We had a drink after Wally made the introductions and ordered supper. Apparently Wally had briefed Dave on my background because he kept watching me with an interest a little strange for an old-time newshound who had been through the mill. Generally nothing fazed those guys and they could talk to presidents and murderers alike without showing a flicker of enthusiasm, but now Dave Severn sat there with the worldly disgust washed out of his eyes and a tight grin of anticipation pulling at the corners of his mouth.

He said, "You really tore things up the last time, Tiger."

"I had to."

"Nothing much reached the papers. That means pull high up on the inside."

I nodded, saying nothing.

"Wally cut me in on some of the details. Too bad it couldn't get printed."

"It's better that way," I told him.

He took a sip of his Martini and grinned at me. "I know why you got that crazy name."

"Wrong, pal. My old man gave it to me. It's for real."

"Still crazy. Now what's going for you?"

"Gabin Martrel," I said.

Wally and Dave gave each other a quick look, serious now.

"You're on touchy ground," Dave informed me. "They have that guy under wraps and he'll stay that way. Nobody gets near him except our intelligence men until he's had everything to say he has to say."

"That's the point, Dave."

"What?"

"Suppose something keeps him from talking. He can still have political asylum without divulging anything important."

"Look, Tiger . . . we're not being given anything yet, but there are ways of putting things together. From what I hear . . . all unofficial sources, of course, is that he's quite willing to speak up."

"Now he is."

Once more the two of them looked at each other and Dave leaned forward on the table. "What are you getting at?"

"Gabin Martrel's name came up once before some years back. Did you check it through?"

"No. Our files had him listed in his official capacities and what items there were concerned his political affairs. There wasn't much because he was always pretty much in the background. The last five years he moved up fast when the Soviets dumped some of their front runners on K's orders. In the last 'silent purge' Martrel emerged as head of the OONA-3 group and was considered responsible for most of the African and Panamanian trouble. I didn't see anything else on him."

"Then you'd better research it a little more, buddy."

"You got an angle, Tiger. What is it?"

"I don't know," I admitted, "but I remember his name coming up."

Severn leaned back, stared at me and nodded. "If it did, I'll find it."

"Good. I'll check in with you tomorrow."

The meal came then and we ate without too much talk. Wally Gibbons seemed nervous, his eyes finding mine for a second occasionally before dropping back to his plate. He was a Broadway reporter who handled the show biz column and the action that came his way was generally limited to movie-star hair pulling in plush pubs or minor scandals along the Stem.

A little after eight we split and when they took a cab across town, I walked over to Broadway, turned south until I reached the street where Ernie Bentley had his new office and took the elevator up to his floor. I didn't worry about catching him in. He was a man dedicated to a job and when he got lost in his work, time meant nothing to him at all.

During the war Ernie had been engaged on the Manhattan Project, pulled out in '46 and went into research chemistry with a major oil company and stayed there until Martin Grady found him and made use of his special inventive talents. A fat salary and a free hand brought more out of him than governmental red tape ever thought possible, and whenever special effects were needed he could be counted on to come up with a beauty.

This time there was no need for deviousness. Among Martin Grady's tremendous assets was listed a going publishing business that featured two major magazines, and what I wanted was a simple press card and some photo equipment.

It took Ernie five minutes to authorize one, check a Leica and a Rollei out of stock with the necessary accessories and have me sign for it. H. Talbot now was a member of the Fourth Estate.

When he handed them over Ernie said, "Central told me to clear you on anything. Got something big going?"

I shrugged. "I don't know."

"Thought you were going to get married today."

"So did I."

"Then it had to be big to cancel the 'I do' routine. Got clearance to wise me up so I can start thinking ahead of time?"

"It's a *Plato* job, Ernie. You're automatically in."

He let out a low whistle. "Three years since the last one. Who is it?"

"Gabin Martrel, the Soviet defector."

"I thought something would show on that. What's the pitch?"

"Nothing yet. He's too hot to handle. I'm playing it by ear until I cut the angle. Somehow he represents a security threat and whatever it is has to be dug out."

"But they got him under wraps at Church Street. Herbie Bender said all he could get was a prepared news release."

"I know."

"Hell," he said, "they gave Martrel more coverage when he and that Lenin Institute skier were in love all over the place during the '56 Olympic games."

I stopped fiddling with the Rollei and stared at him. "That's where I remembered his name from," I said. "Damn, you got a good memory."

"So I'm a sports fan. I was there. Good-looking babe."

"Who was she?"

"Beats me, Tiger. I was interested in the skiing, not the love. I'm too old to go the romance route anymore."

"Lucky for me everybody isn't like that."

"What?"

"Nothing." I was thinking of the personal angle they let come out on Martrel. The one photo had showed a tall, angular guy with thinning hair and a face that reflected years of education and devotion to his peculiar sort of work. He was fifty-two years old, unmarried and a Party member since 1929. Since the war he had come to occupy a powerful, but relatively unknown position in the government until he stood high in the Soviet command with a potential that could lead him to the catbird seat if he pursued his present course of action.

But he was single. And a single man is always a target for a dame. Virgil Adams had a small flash of genius when he tossed the idea at me.

The IATS offices were on the top floor of the Carboy Building on Church Street, a twenty-story edifice housing governmental agencies of seemingly minor importance. Every Washington department seemed to have an annex there, and although IATS was the major factor there, each office, if occupied, was designated as a branch of some service from the Internal Revenue to Military Conscription. A cute cover for the operation, but we knew all about it. Martin Grady's money had bought the information.

Like I figured, I wasn't alone in the lobby at all. Every major wire service had a representative on tap with top men from the local papers ready for any new break in the wall of silence that had been built around Martrel.

A pair of harried IATS clerks were busy making explanations to incoming newsmen, handing out releases that were no more than revised editions of the earlier one and making positive statements that very shortly the government would give out the latest information to the public and to please be patient. They were dealing with the wrong kind of people. Every reporter is impatient, especially when he has to deal with red tape, and twice within thirty minutes the security guards brought out somebody between them who had managed an abortive attempt to get to the top floor.

Finally the sheer weight of numbers put too much pressure on the situation. Three network TV stations were standing by with remote hookups, and half the men inside carried open mikes or portable tape recorders giving out a second-by-second report of the proceedings. Had they allowed any sort of interviews it would have washed out in a hurry after an initial flurry of excitement, but suppressed news became big news because of its suppression and the presence of several Senators flown in from Washington just added to things.

All I could think of was one thing. They were keeping a lid on Martrel, not because he was talking, but because he wouldn't talk.

At ten minutes after midnight the announcement was made that all authorized press representatives would be allowed into the discussion room on the third floor for a press conference with Gabin Martrel and his government protectors. I deliberately picked the middle of the pack that jammed the entrance to the elevator so that when press credentials were presented and inspected by the two guards mine would be scrutinized with less care than if I had been up front.

It worked out the way I planned and I was waved through after being handed a white pasteboard pass that read THIRD FLOOR ONLY ROOM 26. When we got there, each pass was inspected again and we were allowed inside. Like the others, I fought for a front-row position, lost out purposely and took my place in the pack with the Rollei in front of my face, making a show of getting focused on the microphones that were set up and losing myself in the crowd.

Exactly at twelve-thirty, Hal Randolph and a half-dozen others came in, flanking the tall guy in the foreign-cut black suit, and squeezed through to the microphones. Randolph was the relatively unknown head of IATS, and before he could spot me I had the camera up with others, popping flashbulbs as fast as I could fire them, knowing damn well he wasn't going to be spotting me with eyes blinded by the intensity of the lights.

We had had dealings before, and all he'd like to do was break our organization into a million pieces. He had a personal hatred for Martin Grady first, then me, then the entire group. Well, screw him. The guy in front of me turned on a small battery of spots to light the area for his 16-mm. camera, and with those in his face and me behind the lights, I wasn't a bit worried.

The news was brief. The whole thing had been staged simply to satisfy the reporters, let them get some pictures and get the hell out. One of the agency men read a prepared statement that Mr. Gabin Martrel had sought political asylum in this country because he had become disenchanted with Communism, disgusted by the way the Soviets had been turning the world into a battlefield and was firm in his belief that American democracy held the answer to world peace. It was his intention to retire somewhere to a private life and perhaps take up a teaching post in a university if the opportunity presented itself.

While the statement was read I kept watching Martrel. A long time ago he had learned to guard his feelings and his expression was noncommittal. He smiled thinly a few times, nodding in agreement with what was read, but his eyes were playing little tricks on him. They were worried eyes. They had been worried a long time, and despite the years of practice the tiny emotion of fear finally began to show through. He scanned the room in an apparently unconscious manner, but he wasn't fooling me. Martrel was looking. And I couldn't blame him. He was a threat to Soviet security now if the deal was on the square and someplace somebody would be waiting for him. Somehow an attempt would be made to take him out before he could talk, and he was looking for that.

Even though he couldn't see me clearly I knew he had me spotted. He had done the same work before and knew all the tricks. It wasn't my face he saw, but my position of cover behind the lights. His eyes passed over me, then came back, each time dwelling longer in an innocuous way, still looking.

I took the chance that Randolph wouldn't be too wary, deliberately stepped aside faking impatience with the cameraman in front of me, and raised my camera for my own shot. The move seemed to satisfy Martrel because he let his eyes cover other parts of the room from then on.

When the statement was read, Randolph allowed a few questions directed at Martrel and he answered in a deep, direct voice tinged with a Russian accent. The questions were all of a political nature, politely phrased because the reporters knew how quickly the whole affair would be cut off if they got out of hand, and Martrel's answers were as polite and ambiguous as the questions.

During that time I managed to get up close, squeezing

between the cameramen until I had Martrel directly in front of me. When Randolph called the session to a halt there was a sudden babble of annoyed voices, a general hubbub which would continue awhile longer, and I had a chance to say loudly enough just so that Martrel would hear, "Have you found her yet?"

For just a fraction of a second his entire face seemed to freeze. His eyes darted like snakes to my face and the fear was there in its entirety before disappearing behind half-closed lids. He read my face while I was reading his, and as insolently as I could, I raised my camera, took a full head shot of him, nodded and smiled, and backed out through the crowd.

Virgil Adams had been right.

It was a dame.

Enough of us went down together so that I got lost in the pack again, and when I made the street I walked up a few blocks, grabbed a cruising cab and went back to the hotel. As late as it was I picked up the phone, dialed Rondine's apartment and let it ring a good two minutes before I was satisfied she wasn't home.

Hell, I couldn't blame her. You don't blow a woman's wedding day and expect her to take it.

At eight o'clock I met Dave Severn for breakfast in a Broadway restaurant. His face was lined with fatigue and he looked as though he had been up all night. I said, "What was her name, Dave?"

He pulled a folded eight-by-ten Manila envelope from his pocket and passed it across to me. "You're a sharp one, Tiger. It's in there. She's Sonia Dutko, Russian national who defected right after the '56 Olympics. Want me to brief you now?"

"Go ahead. I'll catch up on the details later."

Dave said, "Apparently she and Martrel had been going together for a year or so. He was present at the games and made some of the presentations to his own people. She took two silver medals and presented the picture of the perfectly dedicated Communist. Party member, leader of student groups in the Lenin Institute and all that crap. They must have thought she was A-1 because they didn't keep her guarded like the rest. The night of the big dinner for the participants she simply disappeared, turned up in London, sought out our embassy officials and flew to this country where she obtained the usual political asylum.

"For a while she was a ski instructor in some of the big

lodges in New England, moved out to Sun Valley, then sort of dropped out of sight. Meanwhile, Martrel was catching hell from his superiors behind the Iron Curtain. It was right after that time that he started driving to regain the stature he lost from associating with a known defector and pushed his way to the top. There's a picture of her in there. Take a look. A real cute head."

I flipped the envelope open and took out a series of glossy prints, some taken at the Olympic games, others when Sonia Dutko arrived in this country. She was a cute one, all right, not at all like the robust types that usually came out of the steppes. She seemed to have ash-blonde hair that fell gracefully around a smiling, country-fresh face, and she was built like the proverbial brick outhouse. Even through the heavy European clothes, you couldn't miss the proud look of a body in perfect physical condition, breast high and firm, legs whose curves showed a musculature an artist could hardly duplicate.

"Where is she now?"

Dave shrugged and tugged a cigarette from his pack. "Got me. She just disappeared. Nobody's heard about her since '58. I burned up the wires trying to run her down but no good."

"Still got a lead out?"

"Sure," he told me. "Something'll turn up." He paused, then: "Now, how about you, buddy?"

"My guess is that Martrel defected to find the dame."

"Nuts."

"So it's a guess."

"He's on the spot and you know it. Right now his life isn't worth a nickel so what'll he make if he does find her? You know damn well those people are brainwashed right down the line. With all the broads available to the commissar-type, a guy like Martrel isn't going to toss everything to lay into the one chick who can get his head lopped off. If that was the case he would have done it sooner."

I stuck the envelope in my pocket. "Let's play it from all sides. You never can tell."

"Okay with me. Anything for a story. Wally filled me in on you so it wouldn't surprise me to see you come up with something from left field. Anyway, your obituary will make great reading."

"That's what I like," I said. "Confidence. Are you going to use this little tidbit about the Dutko kid?"

Dave snubbed his butt out and picked up his coffee. "I'll do like everyone else . . . go easy. The word's in with every publisher around to play this cool until Martrel has been handled and has talked. The situation's too tricky to mess with. Besides, I personally don't see any connection."

"Look what Adam did for Eve," I reminded him.

"Sure," he told me quickly, "and look what Delilah did for Samson."

I grinned at his simile, laid down a five on top of the check and told him I'd keep in touch. All the way out the door I could feel his eyes on my back.

At three o'clock I met the three people Newark Control had assigned to me at my request earlier. Hooker and James were medium-sized men, both in their forties, who could get lost in a crowd of two. Hooker had been with me once before and I had heard about James in the General Pacific case. The other was a girl in her late twenties, a mousy thing named Ann Lighter whom Virgil Adams had personally recommended. I gave each one of them a two-by-two head shot I had taken of Gabin Martrel, gave them their basic instructions for staking out the building where they held the guy, with orders to find out where he was living when IATS wasn't questioning him.

Since they had all been well briefed earlier, there wasn't anything further to say. They could contact me directly at the King Leopold or put the information through to Newark where I could obtain it. Each one of them carried enough money to buy any information he needed and they'd all stay on tap until I released them.

When they left I found a pay phone, put a credit-card call to the Raymond Watts Agency in L.A., a group who specialized in tracing missing persons and was authorized to work for us, got Ray himself and told him Sonia Dutko's last known address at Sun Valley. He said he'd check this one out personally and immediately, then I hung up.

I was wondering what kind of snags he was going to hit. If IATS or any of the other Federal agencies recognized the tie-in they'd be at her themselves. What I was betting on was that they'd stay with the political aspect of Gabin Martrel's defection before they branched out.

There was one more call to make.

I dialed Rondine, but instead got a maid. She said that Miss Caine had left some time ago and she didn't know when she was expected back. I thanked her, put the phone back and caught a cab that took me over to the hotel.

All the afternoon papers had a piece in them about Martrel and the TV news carried pictures of the interview. Two of the

tabloids editorialized about the situation, each one harping on
the same theme that seemed to run throughout the news
features. Gabin Martrel was a man who had come to his
political senses at last. In a way he was likened to the earlier
settlers who couldn't stand political oppression in Europe and
migrated here to newfound freedom. It was blandly stated that
he was a repository of secret information and that in time we
would be the beneficiaries of all this knowledge. Almost over-
night, Gabin Martrel had become something of a new American hero.

It was great, though, just how much could be said without
really saying a damn thing at all. One thing I could feel.
Martrel hadn't talked yet. Oh, maybe a little bit to keep
everybody satisfied, but if he was going to open up it was for
a reason. What knowledge he had he'd use as a lever. He was
either playing it smart for the Soviets or wanted that dame.

So far, it had been a quiet day for news. There was a
holdup of a gin mill on Thirty-ninth Street, a three-car colli-
sion with nobody hurt on upper Broadway, an unidentified
body found in the river and a commercial jet holding over
LaGuardia because it couldn't get its gear down. The papers
asked the public to stay away from the airfield until the
situation had been cleared. Jets could still make successful
belly landings.

By now traffic would be thick heading toward LaGuardia
from all directions. Nothing except a hanging could be so
exciting for the morbid public.

Somehow I managed to doze off and awakened when the
phone shrilled next to my head. Ann Lighter identified herself
from the lobby, said she wanted to see me and I told her to
come up. I flicked off the lights, opened the door a couple of
inches and stepped back into the shadowed corner with the
.45 in my hand and waited.

She knew the ropes. She knocked, just once, came in with
both hands in front of her and stood there a moment, then
closed the door and locked it. She still hadn't seen me, but she
knew what I was doing. She felt for the switch, turned it on,
grinned when she saw me stuffing the rod back in my belt and
sat down in the big chair.

"Careful, aren't you?"

"I lost a few friends because they weren't."

Since I had seen her last, she had lost the mousy look.
Virgil Adams had told me she could effect a change to fit the
need, but he hadn't warned me about this. Her hair was down

now so that it framed her face, and the added touches of makeup threw a note of beauty around her features. The other coat she wore hid a body that would have done justice to a Riviera bikini. This one accentuated it. I gave her an approving smile, trying to keep my eyes off her legs, and perched on the end of the bed.

"What did you get?" I asked her.

She didn't refer to notes. None of them do. "Hooker saw them make the exit from another building. Apparently they're connected in some way. James followed them to the Chamberlain House . . ."

"How did he do it?"

"One of our own cabs. He had the OFF DUTY sign down."

"Okay."

"Then he called me. I made the contact there posing as a maid. Gabin Martrel is not registered, but occupies a room on the northeast corner of the ninth floor that is permanently held by the Delta-Phoenix Tool Company. I checked on this organization and as far as I can tell, it's legitimate. They have offices throughout the South and West, four large factories, a registered lobby in Washington and handle government contracts dealing with aero and space equipment."

I nodded, thinking it over. It was a neat setup. "How many are with him?"

"Two in the room; one elevator operator is an agent I recognized who used to be in narcotics with the Treasury Department."

"He's still one of them then."

"One of the maids on that floor is carrying a gun. I'd say she was planted there too."

"Anything else?"

"End of report," she said and crossed her legs. "What do you want me to do now?"

"Stay on tap with Newark Control. From here on it will be my baby. I'll call Virgil and release you and the others. I doubt if I'll need you again, but you can never tell."

Her eyes had a deep greenish tint to them and she looked at me obliquely, a shadow of a smile playing with the corners of her mouth. "Virgil said you might need me now."

"What for?"

"Weren't you supposed to be a bridegroom by today?"

"Hell yes."

"If your singular condition disturbs you after all that anticipation to the point where it could affect your work, I can fill in. Very nicely, if you must know. Better than most."

I couldn't help laughing. She wasn't kidding at all. "Martin Grady sure is nice to his hired hands, but pass the word on that I'm not hurting. I never did and I'm not going to start now. But thanks anyway."

She faked a pout. "I thought I was going to find a tiger."

"Maybe someday, but not now. I don't like duty-bound sex."

"It could be fun. Last chance."

"Only for now is there a last chance, kid. If I want you I'll take you."

"Okay, Tiger Mann," she said. "I'll be looking for your stripes to show someday."

"They'll come out loud and clear," I told her as she left.

It was raining. Damn, it always seems to rain in New **3**
York. Not much—just a gentle sprinkling that can be
disconcerting if you aren't ready for it. But at least
it kept other people off the streets.

You could walk down Broadway, and where the crowd
usually gathered in front of the Metropole and blocked traffic,
there were only a few of the idiots left. Inside, a real slammer
was at the drums and a guy who blew his brains out on pot
ten years ago and graduated to the Big H was blowing a horn.
He was still on H. But these places weren't what I wanted to
see. These were the places left behind. Down a few blocks
and half a street over was the Chamberlain House, and up
there was the guy I really wanted to see.

There was one advantage working with our organization.
Although it was civilian in concept, it was staffed with pros,
and we were financed to such an extent that there was nothing
we couldn't buy and nobody we couldn't outbid. When Martin
Grady had set up an extralegal organization, it was out of
sheer patriotism and total disgust with the way authorized
agencies were forced to operate, hampered by political indeci-
sion, individual greed and absolute stupidity. We were the
biggest and the best, and if somebody didn't do something to
keep it that way the United States would find itself bitten and
chewed to pieces by the heavy-handed slobs on the other side
of the fence.

In this case I used the magic of the buck to get what I
needed. Oscar McDowell was a bell captain in an old established hotel with connections all over town. He had done a
few spots for us before and knew how to operate and with

cash in hand to buy his services he had what I wanted in less than an hour—access to a room on the ninth floor whose occupant was at the theater and not expected back before midnight. I had Ernie Bentley make a duplicate of the extra key and had the original back with the bellboy who had lifted it and all curses off his head in case I was nailed.

When I got to the Chamberlain House I spotted the Fed running one elevator as quickly as Ann Lighter had, waited until he had gone up and stepped into the next one. At the ninth I got off, turned left toward 937, and for once I was in luck. I was heading toward the northeast corner. When I came to the room I fitted the key in the lock, went in and locked the door behind me and looked at my watch. It was twenty-five after ten. In exactly twenty minutes the action should start.

Newark Control had arranged for two men licensed to carry guns and kept handy for such a situation to begin the diversion in the lobby by being spotted by the elevator operator. I hoped they were both good actors. I took a pair of water glasses from under their paper wrappers, filled them and dumped the contents on the bed twice, then called the housekeeper to get a maid in to clean up my accident and sat down behind a paper with the TV going loud.

She took a good six minutes to get there and there was something reluctant about her attitude. It just wasn't that of a hotel maid. Neither was the bulge at her waistline the deliberately blousy uniform didn't quite conceal. For a lady cop she made a lousy housemaid. She was too anxious to get back to her assigned routine and the job of changing the sheets took longer than it should have.

Just before a quarter to eleven I called the desk, asked if the bar was still open and when they told me yes, folded the paper up, tossed a five on the table for the maid and got to the door without her ever having seen my face. As I opened it I saw the tail ends of two guys in a hurry getting in the elevator with drawn guns in their hands.

The next two minutes were the longest in the night. Too soon and Martrel would suspect something. Too late and the pair would be back. When I finally tapped on the door I heard his feet come across the room, the lock snap back and I didn't give him any chance to slam the door shut in my face. I pushed it back with the muzzle of the .45 aimed at his gut and rammed him away with the heel of my hand.

"Hello, Martrel," I said.

He knew me. Oh, he had been a long time in the business and remembering faces was one of his attributes. For one second his face hardened, then a touch of fear was there, not understanding what was happening. "You are from . . ."

"Not of your people. Don't sweat it."

"Then what . . ."

"Have you talked?"

"I don't think . . ."

"The others haven't been thinking either," I cut in. "They don't know what you want yet."

"Who are you?" The fear seemed to thicken his accent.

"A private individual with peculiar obligations. I understand you have information that can neutralize the opposition. You're here looking for terms."

"I haven't asked for any." His eyes darted toward the door.

I shook my head. "Let's say I understand you, Martrel. I've dealt with you people for what seems all my life. So you defected. So you're here now but that doesn't mean you haven't the same affection for your parent country you always had. You're a Soviet national and love the bit. If the choice could have been yours you would have stayed with them, pushing their philosophies all the way. So you defected, but that doesn't mean you're going to turn absolute traitor. What you're hoping for is political asylum here and the time to accomplish your primary aim."

Martrel's eyes narrowed slightly and the look he gave me was direct and accusing. "And what is that?"

"To find Sonia Dutko. The broad you're in love with."

I could see the sweat start to bead up on his forehead and his eyes left mine briefly.

I said, "She's a target. They'll go after her and put the squeeze on you. It's part of their procedure and you damn well know it."

"Then what am I to do?"

"Talk up a storm, buddy. You give them everything they want to know."

His hands grasped each other and twisted aimlessly. Abruptly, he turned his back and walked to the window. "I cannot do that. I refuse. I have asked for political asylum and it has been granted. There is no more I am required to do."

"You want her dead?"

Martrel spun around and his face was shiny with sweat now. "No! No, of course not. There is no reason for her . . ."

"Then you be the target, Martrel. As long as you don't talk, you'll be a big fat target your bunch will be aiming at all the way. Talk and you're worthless except as an example maybe, and I doubt if they'll waste a good assassin going after you. But right now you take a choice... love of that goddamn stupid country of yours or the love of Sonia Dutko. In between and you lose both."

It broke him. It had come too quickly and the decision was too big. He slumped in a chair and covered his face with his hands. When he looked up he said, "I... cannot. I cannot speak."

"Where is she, Martrel?"

He shook his head, his eyes dead. "I... don't know."

"If they realize it's the woman you want, she'll die. They'll hold her until you expose yourself for one single shot, then you get it too."

He looked up, wetting his lips. "If... only I could be sure... she was safe..."

"Our agencies can find her."

"No... they are watched. The Soviet... has agents right ... inside yours. If they find out..."

"I found out, Martrel."

"You are not one of them."

I glanced at my watch. Thirty seconds to go. "If she's safe then you'll talk?"

He watched me, looked at the gun that had never come off his middle, then he finally nodded. "If she's safe," he said.

I let him sit there, circled behind him and before he knew what I was going to do, tapped him in that one sensitive spot behind his ear with the butt of the gun and watched him slump in the chair. Then I shoved the .45 in the sling, walked out, and took the fire exit down two floors before ringing for the elevator.

When I reached the lobby they were still cleaning up the situation with the two Newark had sent out, only now there was a pair of uniformed cops on the scene and everything seemed to be under control. I walked on out without being spotted, grabbed a cab and went back to my hotel.

I called Rondine and there was no answer.

So it was over all right.

The hell with it. But I had said that before.

Without bothering to take off my clothes, I flopped back on the bed and shut my eyes, thinking about tomorrow. *Plato*, Martin Grady had said. A dead call. He had inside information on its importance but not the final answer, and that

I had to find out. If the answer didn't come the red button could be pushed or someplace in a little war the big blast would go off, and then a retaliatory blast someplace else until the whole world was one big mass of atomic fusion.

The knowledge one man had could stop that, or delay it a little, or put the best odds on our side at least.

I didn't hear the knock the first time it came.

When it came again I had the gun in my hand and was beside the door with it cocked in my hand and I flipped the locks open and stepped aside, ready to trigger off a body shot if the picture wasn't right, then I said, "Come in."

The door opened, and in the light from the hall I saw who it was, shut the door, locked it and put the gun in my belt. "Hello, doll," I said to Rondine.

She had seen the gun. She had seen the expression on my face in the shaded light and the consternation was plain in her eyes. "Tiger . . ."

I didn't let her finish. "How did you find me here?"

Her smile was faint and tired as she walked into the room. "An overly zealous desk clerk. He knew you had been trying my number and put it through once more before he went off duty. He simply said a Mr. Talbot at the King Leopold had been calling me and would I like to return the call."

"For such things do people like me die, sugar. How did you come here?"

Rondine sat down and leaned back in the chair. "I wasn't followed. I had training in certain techniques before I came to America, remember?"

"Maybe, kid, but you don't know all the ropes. Any good pro could let you think you got away with it. Now I'm going to have to cut out of this place."

"I'm sorry, Tiger," she said, "but you had called often."

"Forget it." For a second I didn't realize how knife-edge sharp my tone had been and I smiled at her to dull it. Yet the tension was there and she could feel it.

I stood there looking down at her, studying the incredible beauty of this woman I had almost killed not long ago, whom I thought I hated because I thought she was the real Rondine who had almost killed me. Even now I could feel the fire of wanting starting in my belly and it was something I couldn't afford.

"You did me out of my wedding night, Tiger. I had been waiting a long time for that night. For a little while I tried to forget."

"When it comes it will be something to remember. I tried to explain..."

She shook her head slowly, her dark auburn hair tumbling in soft waves around her face. "You have something to take its place. You can forget for a little while. I can't."

"Look, kid..."

"Before you do what you have to do, I want my wedding night."

"Rondine..."

"I know what's going to happen. I saw it happen once and I know other things about you now I didn't know before." She smiled gently, stood up with the gracefulness of some big, lovely feline animal and very slowly shrugged out of the belted trench coat.

Beneath it, all she had on was a sheer black nightgown she had saved for this one night and the static attraction of nylon for flesh draped it around her like skin so that even the pulsation of her heart was visible. The perfect symmetry of her breasts rose proudly over the tautness of her stomach and when she turned and walked to the bed the sway of her hips and the curve of her thighs was a grand invitation of love.

She pulled the spread back, sank down and let her head fall back on the pillow, her eyes watching me languidly. I knew what it would be like, the wild excitement, the unbelievable fury of it all, because once to save her I had had her. Now she wanted me to have her again and knew, like the last time, she could make it so I couldn't refuse.

I walked over, touched her face, knowing what I was going to do.

Then the phone rang.

"Leave it," she said.

I picked it up. "I can't," I told her, and into the phone: "Talbot here."

"Ray Watts, Tiger. You told me to call when I had something," he said. "You clear there?"

"Go ahead, Ray."

"We picked up the Dutko woman's trail from Sun Valley then into L.A. She changed names four times along the way. For a while she worked with an optical company connected with the picture business, then went with L. G. Productions as a technical advisor under the name of Helen Wells."

"Why did she change her name?"

"Best we could figure was she didn't want publicity or any

connection with the past. She did get quite a lot of attention for a few years."

"She have a family in Russia?"

"Apparently not. That was one reason she could afford to cut out."

"Where is she now?"

"A week ago they wrapped up a picture and she said she was taking a vacation. A woman answering her description took the 11:05 jet out of L.A. nonstop for New York last Wednesday. My guess is that she's in your backyard somewhere. You want me to pick it up out there?"

"No. It'll save time if I work it myself."

"Okay. Now look . . . I checked on her friends. She had a few close ones who visited her regularly at Sun Valley for the skiing and they all spoke a foreign language. presumably Russian. She had a great affection for the mother tongue so I'd check the native quarters, if you know what I mean."

"I get the picture."

"While she was there she worked with one of the hotel pros who was an archer. She got to be an expert at it in a matter of weeks. A natural athlete. You might check that angle."

"Got it. Any political affiliations?"

"I'm outthinking you, buddy. I looked into that bit and there was nothing. From what I uncovered she was approached by a few groups who wanted to use her defection for their own advantages, and she wouldn't have anything to do with them. In fact, she applied for her first citizenship papers."

"Under what name?"

"Her own."

"Address?"

"165 Chuenga in L.A."

"Is she expected back?"

"L. G. Productions starts a new picture two months from now and she's scheduled to be on it. Something to do with the Olympics. Besides being a technical advisor she's doubling for the star. I understand they would have used her except that the star was already committed, and besides. she's one of those rare types who doesn't have a desire to be a famous actress."

I could have thought of another answer, but I didn't mention it.

Ray said, "Bill Copely was instructed to pick up the trail in New York in case I couldn't reach you, and you can contact him at our office there. By now he may have a lead. He's got an apartment on East Seventieth."

"Good, Ray. I'll call him now."

I hung up, took out the phone book and looked up the Watts Agency in the city. I didn't expect an answer and got none. The next number was Copely's home number and on the second ring somebody picked up the phone. The voice was guarded and said, "Yes?"

"Bill Copely, please."

"Who's speaking?"

"Never mind, it's agency business. Put Bill on."

"Sure, but . . ."

"Forget it, friend," I said and cradled the phone. Just to be sure I dialed Wally Gibbons at his office, found him on tap for once and asked him if there was anything doing at Copely's address.

It didn't take him long at all. The paper had already had a call on it. There was a suicide by gas at the address and the guy's name was William Copely. Age thirty-six, unmarried and employed by the Raymond Watts Agency with headquarters in Los Angeles. He had more, but I just thanked him and stopped it there.

"You have to go again," Rondine said.

"The choice isn't mine, kid," I said.

I couldn't look at her. I grabbed my coat and hat, climbed into them, made sure I had a couple of extra clips for the .45, picked up the Rollei and the camera case and left. As I closed the door I heard her sob once, then I was back on the edge of the jungle again.

Outside the apartment a couple dozen people were **4**
gathered, some in pajamas and bathrobes, others in
clothes hurriedly thrown on. A uniformed patrolman
and a fireman were insisting they stay evacuated until the gas
had been cleared. None of them was enjoying the situation
and the usual curious weren't helping things any.

I used my press card to get past the police lines and inside
the lobby. The cop on duty nodded when I flashed my wallet
and said, "Second floor. You're dragging in late. Most of the
others have gone already."

"Ah, I was on another call," I told him casually and walked
on up.

The door of Apartment 2-C was wide open and so were the
windows at both ends of the hall but I could still smell the
traces of gas. I walked on in, waved to the reporters taking
down the details from a detective and went out to the kitchen
where the body was lying on the floor covered by a sheet. A
pair of attendants from the morgue wagon downstairs were
getting ready to lift it onto a stretcher. Two firemen and
another detective were standing by, laughing at something,
totally oblivious to death so close at hand. It was an old story
to them.

I said, "Can I take a look?"

One cop shrugged, nodded and went on talking. An atten-
dant flipped the sheet back so I could get a look at what was
left of Bill Copely. He wasn't very pretty. None of them is, like
that. He was on his back right beside the gas stove, with a
pillow under his head and both hands folded across his chest.
"Funny how they like to be comfortable when they decide to

kick off," the guy said, pointing to the pillow. "Had two like that last week. One even got a haircut and shave then dressed up in his best clothes to save the undertaker trouble."

"Thanks."

He pulled the sheet back, and what was left of Copely went on the stretcher. The detective who had been talking to the fireman walked over and said, "No pictures?"

"Not worth it. What happened?"

"One of the tenants smelled the gas and called in. The guy had been dead too long to revive. Same old story."

I pulled a sheaf of papers and a pencil out and looked at the cop.

"William Copely," he said. "His personal papers listed him as an insurance investigator with the Watts Agency. He comes from California originally, I think. None of the neighbors knew too much about him, and we haven't located anybody from his office yet."

"Know why he did it?"

"Sure." He reached over to the table and picked up a letter. There was no envelope. "A *Dear John* note from some dame named Flo. She broke her engagement and married some joker she suddenly fell in love with. He had it in his hand when we found him."

He let me see the note, a one-page affair on plain, cheap stationery. There was no date and no address and the letter had been folded and refolded a dozen times.

I handed it back. "Tough."

"Nothing new. He stretched out, plugged up the window and turned on the oven and the top burners. Took the trouble to blow out the pilot first or we could have had a hell of a blast up here. What he forgot was to turn off the TV set. That could've done it as well as lighting a cigarette. These nuts don't give a damn how many they take with them usually. Me, I prefer they jumped into a back alley. It's safer all around."

I took down what details there were, listed the names of the officers in attendance and said, "Mind if I take a look around?"

"Help yourself. Nothing much here. Just the usual clothes a bachelor keeps on hand and not enough in the refrigerator to feed a cat. He's only been here three months and most likely ate out all the time. Probably the first time he used the stove."

It didn't take long to get a good picture of Bill Copely. Typical bachelor probably described him as well as anything, but with the kind of background he would have had to have to work for Ray Watts, I wasn't holding with any suicide. Everybody Ray had in his organization was an ex-cop or former intelligence personnel selected for their stability.

Scattered on the floor around the dumbwaiter and the windows were the folded newspapers used to seal up the openings and they were the only things out of place. Everything else was Army-style neat. In the bedroom his watch, a handful of change and an open billfold with the edges of money sticking out of it lay on the dresser, but the bed was tightly made, and except for the missing pillow, untouched.

It was a two-room apartment with the bathroom off the bedroom. The living room was combined with the kitchen and furnished with a couple of big chairs, a couch and a breakfast table with four metal and plastic chairs. There were two small pillows at one end of the couch and when I edged by it I saw three pennies lying between the cushions.

I put the note sheets in my pocket, said so long to the cops and walked to the door. The other tenants were filing back up, each trying for a peek in the apartment as they went by, all still complaining about being herded out of their homes.

The cop said, "Finished?"

"Nothing here."

"That's what the other guys said. Can't always get a story."

"I'll wait."

Just before I left I checked the door where the lock had been smashed out of its socket by the cops who broke it open. The cop said, "They did it the quick way. Good thing it wasn't one of those steel fireproof jobs like in the newer places."

"Didn't he plug up the door?"

"Hell, they always forget something."

"They sure do," I said.

At the corner cigar stand I contacted Newark Control and got Virgil Adams. I told him I wanted Ann Lighter, Hooker and James again to backtrack the movements of Bill Copely and gave him a rundown on what I had seen. He could get it in his initial report to Central and save me the time. I told him I'd be shifting hotels and would contact him later for the report.

I went in the side entrance of the King Leopold Hotel, checked for any possible stakeouts and when I found none, took the elevator up to my room. I stuck the key in the lock and pushed it open, flipping the light on at the same time. Rondine wasn't there now.

But I had company. Three of them. Quiet men who sat there watching me, not smoking, silent, and one had a gun in his hand.

Hal Randolph said, "Come on in, Tiger."

And Thomas Watford said, "Please do, Mr. Mann."

Both of them were heads of IATS, and when they went to such personal lengths to process a case you knew the heat was on. The other one I hadn't seen before, but his type was typical. CIA, IATS or some other agency. He was the one with the gun.

Randolph let me sit down, then nodded to the young guy and he put away his gun. "Who's your friend?" I asked.

"Cutter. Albert Cutter. Although you've never met, he's quite familiar with your history."

I glanced at him, watching the diffident way he sat there. He was about thirty and probably rugged under the conservative-cut gray suit he wore. All the earmarks of education, breeding, intelligence and training were there.

"Perhaps I can tell you this, Mann," Randolph said. There was a tight look of pleasure on his face. "Since we weren't able to get Congressional action on your group and Martin Grady had the influence and money to defer the proceedings, the committee has arranged to have your organization under constant scrutiny and continuously investigated."

"Don't you mean harassed, buddy?"

"Your interference isn't welcome, Mann."

I grinned at him. "Tough. Somebody has to do something to straighten out the mess you people leave sometimes."

"The political aspect . . ."

"Balls!" I snapped to my feet and stared him down. "I'm tired of the crap that goes on. A lot of us are and that's why we work the way we do. This country wasn't founded on a goddamn octopus government that lets mice like Castro and Kremlin bums pick us apart. This is a civilian country, Randolph, and you'd damn well better remember it. When something gets screwed up and the striped-pants boys can't handle it and the politicos are scared to death to touch it for fear of stepping on somebody's toes and maybe not getting reelected, then we do something about it.

"Now remember this, all you guys, and pass it around. Nobody's stopping us. We'll stick our noses in when we think it's needed and do what you're supposed to do. If somebody has to get knocked off to ease a situation then we're happy to do it. We're all trained pros and you guys could learn a lot from any of us. We've hauled your ass out of the fire plenty of times and lost a lot of good guys doing it. Nobody's stopping us. Nobody. Now get to the point or blow."

For a minute I thought both Randolph and Thomas Watford *would* blow. Both looked tight enough to pop and their faces were flushed with anger. Only Cutter sat there calmly, and he seemed to be smiling.

Finally Randolph said, "Well, maybe we can stop *you* right now, Tiger. Maybe we can cut *you* out of the action."

"How?"

I knew what he was going to pull, and if he made it he could do what he wanted to. "You invaded a hotel room at the Chamberlain."

"How about that?"

He ignored me and went on, "Gabin Martrel gave us an accurate description and identified a photo of you. The elevator operator did the same. Martrel was being held there until his official political asylum was confirmed; meanwhile, he was a ward of the government and your act was a violation of certain statutes."

"You'll have a hell of a time proving it."

"Nevertheless, we can hold you long enough to slow down whatever you think you're going to do."

"It will make cute reading in the papers."

"We can afford that chance."

"Maybe," I said.

Randolph grinned viciously. "Suppose we try, Mann. A few days in the cooler will do you good."

But I could grin too. "You haven't asked me yet."

Randolph lost his expression and scowled. "What?"

"What you came for. Why are we interested in Martrel?"

"All right, why?"

"Because he's not going to talk to you people and I think you know it. He's going to keep all that information bottled up tight, and we'll be sitting on a gold mine without being able to get in the door. He doesn't even have to worry about it. You can't do a damn thing to make him talk."

I had him nailed there and he knew it. His mind was checking all the facts against all the angles and trying to make the odds work for him. He said, "And I suppose you can?"

"There are ways."

"We know of some of your ways. You left quite a trail behind you in several places. Dead men and broken people."

"But they talked. They had done the same things to others themselves. Feel as sorry about it as you would for Hitler."

"You won't do that here."

I looked at them all a long moment. "I don't have to."

Watford sat back and crossed his arms, his attitude casual now. "What *are* you interested in, Tiger?"

"The same thing you are."

"Unless you give us a little more you won't be around for a few days."

They weren't kidding. So now I could throw them a bone. I said, "A guy died tonight, an apparent suicide by gas. His name is Bill Copely and he's an investigator for the Watts Agency. Nobody knows what he was working on, but he may have stumbled across something concerning Martrel. I'd say you check the door lock for a forced entry with a pick and look over the body for a possible hypo injection of some sedative that would keep him out cold until the gas killed him. An autopsy might show what was used, but it had better be a good one or the gas will disguise it. I'd say the killer opened his door, smothered him with a pillow until he was unconscious, injected him, then set the scene for an apparent suicide."

All three of them passed those small glances back and forth, trying to make something out of what I told them.

"Do the police know this?" Watford asked.

"I didn't bother to ask. I was on the premises in an official capacity of a reporter. Getting that information is their business."

"Then how did you make contact with this Copely? Had you known him?"

"Nope. He called me and said he had something I might be interested in concerning the guy. He gave me his name and address, but when I got around to dropping in he was already dead."

"But you went as a reporter," Randolph said easily. "You were using a cover."

"I always do, friend. I'm not in a position to take too many chances. I never know what I'm going to run across. Now why don't you find out about it?"

Randolph got up and went to the phone.

I said, "I'm going to shower while you find out. Mind?"

"Go ahead."

I took my time about it, making plenty of noise in the shower, dried off and climbed into my shorts. When I came out Randolph was just hanging up the phone. "How'd you make out?"

Quietly, he said, "They found a needle mark on his thigh."

"Okay, then there's your starting point. Now you know as much as I do."

Thomas Watford got up and Cutter followed him. "I wonder. If you're wrong we'll come back to you again."

"How'd you find me this time . . . keep a check on Edith Caine?"

Watford smiled grimly and nodded. "Yes . . . your Rondine. She wasn't clever enough to shake Cutter here. I advise you to stay around town."

"I intend to, gentlemen. Now if you'll scram, I'll hit the pad."

They went by me and only Cutter bothered to nod good night. He was all pro and he knew another one when he saw one. I winked and locked the door after they left.

But I didn't go to bed. I packed my stuff, made sure the corridor was cleared and walked all the way down the fire exit to the lobby. It wasn't too hard to check out quietly, not when you tip the bellboy ten bucks to do all the work for you. I switched to the Brigham Hotel under my own name of T. Mann, address, Columbia, S.C., called Ray Watts from a pay station and told him what happened to Bill Copely and not to mention the Martrel assignment. If there were questions it was something he picked up himself.

Ray got the picture fast and said he'd take care of it. What bothered him was that Copely hadn't left anything around in the way of a report. I know it wouldn't have done any good to shake the place down. If the killer had time he would have found anything Copely left behind and that was that. When I hung up I went back to the hotel and fell into bed. It had been a long day. I told Newark Control where I was and went to sleep.

She could have called first. But she didn't. Instead, she knocked on the door at twelve noon, broke me out of a crazy dream scrambling for the .45 beside my bed, and when I opened the door she stood there smiling and at first I didn't recognize her. This time the mousy broad was a dream in a fitted suit and cape with her hair all blonde and piled on top of her head. Ann Lighter was either the damndest woman I ever saw or a master of feminine disguises.

I said, "Come on in. So I'm not dressed."

"With that gun in your hand you're a perfect cover for a certain magazine."

"Great."

She shut the door behind her and walked into the room. "Can't Grady Enterprises afford better accommodations? I think I'm making more than you are." Ann smiled at me and eased herself into a chair. "And stop being surly."

"I just got up."

"Obviously. But I thought a man of your talents never slept alone."

"A misconception, kid. What's going?"

She shook her head and made a face at me. "They told me how you were. I didn't really believe it. How stands the Union, Tiger?"

"Firm, sound and rockbound, doll. Now get with it." I reached for my pants and shirt, pulled them on and she didn't bother watching. It's one benefit of being old enough to pick your own time and place. This dame could bother me without knowing it and she'd better watch herself. One day she'd make the wrong move or say the wrong word at the right time and she was going to be treated to something that never happened before and wouldn't happen again. Maybe.

Like the pro she was, though, she switched characters in a hurry. She said, "From the top or shall I rough it in?"

"Only essentials."

"Fine. We ran it through Central to get all the b.g. and here's what came out. Your friend Ray Watts assigned Copely to picking up the Dutko trail. He checked the airport and located a woman fitting her description traveling under the name of Helen Bell. We got lucky when one of the stewardesses gave us a definite make because she recognized her. No trouble with the name change because the girl knew of her history and thought she wanted anonymity. She took a cab from the airport . . ."

"Find the driver?"

"Certainly. He dropped her off at the Shrevesport Hotel in the upper Thirties and there the trail ends. She didn't check in, nor did anyone of her description."

"That's a lot of work for one night."

"This is a *Plato Operation*," she reminded me.

"Check out the nearby hotels?"

"All of them."

"Cabs?"

"As many as possible. We're not done yet. Hooker and James are on it now."

"Bill Copely?"

"Nothing on him at all. Either he picked up her trail and followed it farther or he gave up at that point too and went home. The latter is my guess."

I reached for the phone book, found the Shrevesport, then looked it up in the Yellow Pages. It was a hotel for women only, and most likely one of those places run like dormitories for new girls in the city to park while they find jobs and get relocated.

"Sonia Dutko never went that cheap," I told her.

"That's what we thought. My guess is that she simply told the driver to go there and switched cabs."

"Where's Hooker and James now?"

"Checked in the Taft. One will be sleeping, the other still going."

"I'll see how far they went. Any cover names?"

"No."

"Good. What are you planning?"

She grinned at me, stood up and flipped off the cape. Very deliberately she started to climb out of her suit. "I'm for the hot bed routine, Tiger. Me . . . I haven't had time to find a pad so I'm going to stay here and sleep it out. Mind?"

"Be my guest," I said.

Before I could get my coat on she had shrugged out of her blouse and I wondered what the hell ever made me think she was the innocuous, mousy type. She was one of the fullest-bosomed women I had ever seen, with eyes that were all daredevil, and the grin she threw at me was one big, fat challenge. I didn't want to see anymore and she didn't make it easy for me.

But just to play the game I looked back appreciatively as her fingers found the zipper on her skirt and said, "Don't waste the routine, sugar."

Her laugh was light and throaty. "Your stripes aren't showing yet, Tiger."

"When they do you'll scream," I said.

"Loud?"

"They'll hear you all over the place."

"I can hardly wait," she told me and rolled into the bed naked.

But it was that simple thing of seeing the metamorphosis of a woman that made me think of what could have happened.

I grabbed a cab to the Shrevesport Hotel and went in to the desk where a pair of formidable matron types defended the bastion against all males. They looked up at me with hostile eyes that meant they saw *man* and all *man* was evil.

The one with the tightly wound gray hair said, "Yes?" and waited.

"I'd like to see your register for the night before last."

"Why?"

"I'm looking for a party. It's possible she didn't use her right name."

Her smile was a tight, sardonic thing. "I'm sorry, but that is not possible."

Too many guys have been buffaloed by the type. Too many guys remembered an overpowering matriarchy and domestic authority and have fallen from just the look she gave me. I was lucky. These types never were a threat. If they wanted something turned on they knew the right way to do it.

I leaned on the counter as insolently as I could and when she read my face she read it right. I said, "How would you like some big trouble?"

"See here . . ."

"Shut up. Just answer me."

"If you think . . ."

"I think I can break your mouth real fast and being a broad won't stop me. I think I can find ways to get this place rousted in a hurry, and if you want to try it, kid, it's your play."

There was no hostility in her eyes now. She was just plain scared. I looked over at the other one. "And touch that phone and you'll see it happen. Play it right and it will end now."

Both of them became tired old ladies at once, licking their lips nervously, waiting for the other to do something and neither being able to move. Finally the one nodded, pulled a card file from under the counter and put it in front of me.

There had been nine reservations picked up that night. Four gave married names, but the others left out any reference to their status. One by one I held them out and asked for a description. It took the both of them to remember, but they got through the list. Three of them answered the description of Sonia Dutko except for one thing. Two were brunettes and one a redhead. No ash blondes had checked in.

But this was the era of quick-change wigs and a woman didn't need too much more to change her personality. I memorized the room numbers, put a fifty on the counter to soften things for the old gals and shoved the cards back to them. "Thanks for the cooperation. I'd advise you to forget you ever saw me. Got it?"

I stood there until they both nodded jerkily, and when one picked up the bill I knew I was forgotten.

But outside I wasn't forgotten. I felt the tug across the side of my coat and even though there was no sound I knew a bullet had come from someplace out of the night, and I took a running dive toward the parked cars at the curb, reaching for the .45 in the sling. Right behind me something slapped the pavement and ricocheted off into the night as I scrambled between the cars and crouched there.

Both shots had come from my left out of a silenced gun, but I hadn't seen the flash and couldn't spot the position of the gunman. I knew it wasn't from a window because the angle the second shot ricocheted from was too flat.

Right then a burst of laughter came from one of the buildings and a dozen teen-agers came out squealing and poking one another, and the street took that time to get busy. Two cabs pulled up, let out customers, a squad car went by, the driver just starting to lean on the siren button to answer some distant call, and a few more people turned the corner and started walking toward me.

Slowly, I got up, stuck the gun away, edged along the cars and started west toward the avenue.

Two points had been proven this night. Sonia Dutko was in that building and *they* were after her. Grab her as a hostage and Gabin Martrel would never talk.

The other point was that I was still on the Soviet "A" list and had been recognized. Now we had to see who could get to her first.

They'd move fast now that they knew I had a line **5**
on her. Most likely they'd call in for orders, but if
they had to they'd move in with strength and get her
out the hard way.

I hated to cause the city all the trouble, but there was no
other effective way of sealing off the building. I found a phone
a few stores down, dialed the fire department, sounded as
hysterical as I could when I told them smoke was pouring out
of an upper rear window of the Shrevesport Hotel and hung
up. To double the action I pulled the switchbox on the corner,
crossed over and waved down a cab, hopped in and told him
to take me to the Brigham. Before we had gone two blocks I
heard the hooters on the engines coming from across town and
grinned to myself. Besides the fire department there would be
cops on the scene, and some of them would stick around to
investigate the incident, and nobody was going to be moving
in on anybody until they had cleared out.

She never heard me come in. She was sprawled out face-
down on the bed with the covers only partly covering her,
completely relaxed in a deep sleep, her clothes in a heap on the
chair beside her. I sat on the edge of the bed and ran my
finger down the line of her spine, then rubbed the back of her
neck until she moved unconsciously, a small smile of pleasure
on her face.

"Ann . . ."

She *hummed* softly and I raked my nails down her back.
"Hey kid. Wake up."

Like a kid, she drew her legs up and squirmed onto her

side. I grinned, poked a knuckle against her ribs and said,
"Reach!"

She came awake fast then, her eyes popping open into a
slitted glare of sudden consternation at having been caught
with her guard down, and in that one moment of half sleep
that she didn't recognize me there was nothing but professional
hate there.

Then she saw me and said, "Damn it . . ."

"Sorry, kitten. Had to rouse you. I've got Sonia Dutko
located and need you."

Ann Lighter bounced out of the bed totally unconcerned
with the lovely nakedness of her body, and reached for her
clothes, fully awake now. While she got dressed I went to the
window and looked down at the street below. Even at that
hour the city was like an octopus, with weaving tentacles of
lights reaching down every row of buildings as if looking for a
victim.

"What happened?"

"She's in the Shrevesport, all right. She must have had a
dark wig with her and went in under a phony name. Three fit
her description, Roberts in 511, Hopkins in 300 and Grace in
434. She's being watched from outside and whoever is there
took a couple of shots at me. I pulled the firebox and the
place will be locked in tight for a while with nobody going in
or out, especially men, so I want you to get down there."

She nodded.

"Check in as an out-of-towner and see if you can get to
those three. You'll recognize her if you see her."

"Are you sure the one watching wasn't a woman too?"

"I'm taking the chance that it wasn't. If it was they won't be
able to move before you do anyway. I'll cover you from the
outside and if I can figure a way in I'll do it."

"I have the picture. You can turn around now."

She had finished dressing, but in those few minutes she had
done something with her hair and the shape of her face that
made her a perfect resident for a woman's hotel. She had
reversed the cape and the suit jacket and with it went the full-
blown look, the beauty and the challenge that was pure sex.
She was back to the mousy type again.

"You should have been an actress," I told her.

"I was," she said.

"Then why go into the gun game?"

She smiled, walked over and patted my cheek. "It's a long
story, Tiger. I'd like to tell it to you in private sometime."

"I'd like to hear it." She let the smile fade slowly, then said, "Any special instructions?"

"Don't expose yourself to anything. Remember, I'm going to be close by. See if you can get Sonia Dutko out of there without being spotted. There has to be several exits in that place."

"I can manage."

"You know of a safe place to keep her?"

"Perhaps you'd better pick a spot."

I grabbed a piece of stationery, jotted down the address of a rooming house I had used before that was in a sleazy section of the city, but whose owner liked Martin Grady's money. I wrote in the code word that was authorization for admittance and signed my name. When I handed it to her I said, "The super knows the angles here. Just give him that."

She took the note, folded it and stuck it down the cleft of her breasts in a natural pocket and nodded. "Give me a five-minute start," she said.

"Right."

Down in the lobby I picked up a paper and scanned through it, waiting for the time to pass. On page two was a six-inch single column headlining Gabin Martrel. He had been taken to City General Hospital with a minor gastric complaint and was being kept there under observation. I read it over carefully, but it had all the noncommittal earmarks of a pre-pared statement for the press.

Keeping Martrel in the hospital could be a cute way of holding him under strict observation with a police guard.

Or it could be something else.

I dug out a dime, pulled the phone listing for Thomas Watford, Imports-Exports out of my memory and dialed the number. When I identified myself to a male voice, Watford got on, his tone guarded. "What do you want, Mann?"

"Information."

"Then I suggest you come here."

"Your tail lose me?"

He cursed softly under his breath.

I said, "The autopsy checked out Bill Copely's murder, didn't it?"

"We want to speak to you about that."

"No doubt. First I want some information." When he didn't answer, I said, "How was Martrel poisoned?"

"Tiger . . ."

"Look, buddy. I gave you Copely. Okay, so you lack a

motive except that I suggested a tie-in with Martrel. You tell me what I want to know and maybe I'll give you a starting point."

"Goddamn it, Mann..."

"Quit trying to trace the call, feller. I'll be out of here in thirty seconds anyway. Answer me."

He took a few seconds, then chanced it. "Somebody got to his food. We haven't any leads except that the room-service waiter stopped a few moments to give directions to a couple of guests that went unidentified. One of them could have distracted him while the other dosed the sandwiches."

"How is he?"

"Martrel'll live. Now let's hear from you, Tiger."

"Shortly," I said and hung up.

It took fifteen minutes to get back to the Shrevesport, and the last of the fire trucks were just pulling away, leaving a red sedan with a battalion chief and his driver and two squad cars there. One of the cops was talking to a few people, looking for witnesses but not getting anywhere. Half the time anybody who pulls a firebox likes to stick around and watch the action, so I knew anyone in the vicinity would be questioned; I just beat them to the punch.

I hated to wear out my press card, but it was a direct approach and not likely to arouse suspicion. I got to the uniformed driver of the red sedan, flashed the wallet but got a negative sign from him.

"False alarm. Nothing at all."

"Pull the box?"

"Yeah... called in, too. Different approach. Usually it's just the box."

One of the cops walked over with the chief and I flipped the wallet at them again. The cop said, "Might as well go on home. Another phony."

"Any leads?"

"Naw. This is the second this week in this neighborhood. It's either drunks or kids."

"Hell, now that I'm here I might as well do a story on that. Might rate a column with the proper approach. That's a hotel for women, isn't it?"

"Strictly. A man couldn't get out of the lobby. With those two old biddies guarding the place you don't even need a moat."

I nodded, then said, "You talk to the residents?"

"No, why?"

"Just thought of something. Dames do some screwy things when they get cabin fever. Suppose one of them wanted to liven things up a little just to see some men around."

Both the chief and the cop exchanged glances. "It's a thought," the chief said. "We had one like that in a place for old retired couples last year."

"Want to check it out?" the cop asked him.

"Hell yes, I do," the chief agreed.

"Mind if I come along?"

"No. Come on. A little publicity might put a lid on this crap. Especially when somebody winds up in the can."

I kept my back to the desk and talked to one of the cops while the chief did the explaining at the desk. He was mad enough not to take any back talk from the two old gals and told them to stay put and not call any of the rooms. One cop stayed at the front door and another was instructed to go around the back in case the questioning started somebody running.

We took each room as they came up and went through the entire routine. It took time, but there was no way I could rush it without getting out of line. There were only three rooms I was interested in: 300, 434 and 511. An hour and a half later we reached 300 and met the Roberts woman. She fitted Sonia Dutko's description all right if you read it off a sheet, but her face could stop a clock and she had a solid American accent.

By the time we reached the next floor I tapped the cop on the arm and said, "We can cut it shorter if I took some rooms on my own instead of following you guys around."

Impatience got the better of them. The chief waved me on, and I went up the corridor to the first turn and started on the even numbers. I hit six rooms with all the questions and then I came to 434. I knocked and there was no answer. After I stood there thirty seconds tapping repeatedly, I looked at the maid who was watching me timidly from inside a linen closet and said, "Open it."

She didn't question me at all. She had been watching every move we made like everybody else and wasted no time. She turned the key in the lock and scurried back to her closet again.

I didn't find the girl who had signed in under the name of L. Grace.

But I did find Ann Lighter. She was lying on the floor with her head twisted at an ugly angle and death in her eyes. She stared at the wall with a look of concentrated horror, her face suffused and one terrible bruise discoloring the side of her neck.

Death lay at my feet too often to be a stranger to me, but this time I couldn't help the rage that filled me up. For one second I went tight as a drum and wanted to tear somebody apart and throw the pieces in the gutter, then I came back again. Fast.

I felt her skin and there was hardly any warmth left. It only took a second to find the .25 automatic she carried in a supple leather holster, and I slipped it off and dropped it in my pocket. Then I felt for the note I had given her.

The note was gone. The window was unlatched and outside was a fire escape.

I didn't bother going through her bag. There wasn't that much time and I knew she wouldn't have anything tying in our organization anyway. Whatever she carried would only be cover identity and nothing would be traced to us. I went back outside, touching nothing, whistled both the cop and the chief to the room and when they came up I said, "Inside."

Until the policeman went through his routine, I didn't move. He glanced up from the body, said, "Touch anything?" and I shook my head.

"What happened?"

I told him, then called the maid in to corroborate my story. She took one look at the body on the floor and went into a dead faint that choked off her scream.

"Look," I said, "you want me to call this in or should I wait? I can get a scoop on this bit."

"It'll come out anyway," the chief said. But at least he appreciated my asking.

Deliberately, I moved toward the phone. The cop said, "Don't touch that!"

"Sorry. I'll use the one in the lobby. Want me to buzz headquarters for you?"

The cop shook his head. "No. I'll do it from the next room. The old dame there will be happy to hear the news."

And I left as easily as I came. Only now I knew one thing. Somebody else was going to die with a broken neck when I found him. Or her. And *her* looked like Sonia Dutko. I couldn't quite picture any man getting in that place, and if the Dutko doll was an Olympic athlete she could have had the strength to break Ann's neck. Well, she wouldn't be the first woman I had knocked off.

I got back to the Brigham and called Newark Control, then

sent a report directly in to Martin Grady. Another call got Hooker and James and off the chase. From now on it was my baby all the way and I didn't want anybody to touch it. Two were dead, one had been poisoned and one was missing and *Operation Plato* was well on the way. *Kill or be killed. The security of this country was at stake.*

But screw the security or the "be killed" angle. All I could think about was how nice it would feel to have somebody's neck under my hands who had killed Ann Lighter, and I knew that whatever it took, I'd find that person. I went to sleep dreaming about it.

The morning papers had Ann listed as a Mrs. Romero from Paterson, New Jersey. She had checked into the Shrevesport, been assigned to room 727, and so far no connection between the missing Grace woman and Mrs. Romero had been established. The police assumed that the assailant had been a man, but there was a denial of any male on the premises by the women who ran the hotel, except for the few who came to call in the lobby and whose movements were carefully scrutinized. All had been in plain sight, all had been observed leaving, and the murder was still up in the air.

I flipped the pages of the paper over, found nothing, then picked up a tabloid and found another summary of the kill that had little more to say but dwelt on the feminine aspect of the Shrevesport and hinted at the possibility of a homosexual angle.

On page four, though, I found something else. The body that had been recovered from the river earlier was that of a seaman named Clement Fletcher and an autopsy showed that he had been dead drunk after making the rounds of a half-dozen waterfront saloons and had probably fallen from the dock when he was trying to get back on board his ship to sleep it off.

Great. Scratch one little guy who would never get to Perdes with his Geiger counter. In one shot I had lifted all his hopes, and he tried to drown his troubles in booze and only succeeded in drowning himself. It would have been better if I had never butted in to save his roll that time down in Panama.

Damn it, everything I went near was turning up dead.

Including a marriage.

I rammed the paper into a wad and threw it against the

wall as the phone rang. I said, "Yes," and my voice sounded coarse and raspy.

"This is . . . Mr. Tiger Mann?" The woman on the other end had a strange inflection.

Instead of identifying myself I said, "Who is this?"

"Tiger Mann?" she insisted.

"Yeah. Speaking."

"This is . . . Sonia Dutko." Her voice was hesitant, fearful and she spoke as though she didn't want to be overheard. I sucked in a deep breath, then I was all right again and it was business with no personal involvement. So Ann Lighter was dead. Now let's see what this was about.

"Where are you?" I asked her.

"Your friend . . . the woman . . . she gave me name of place and a paper to give a person there. I go there. I read the paper where in my room at the hotel is found a dead woman. I think it is your friend."

"How did you know where to reach me?" I asked her.

She said, "From the paper. It had the name of your hotel. On the bottom was your name." She paused and I could hear her breathing. "I am afraid to go back. I do not know what to do."

"Where are you now?"

"At this place from the paper. I call from here."

"Stay there. Don't talk to anybody and let no one in your room until I get there. If you want anything to eat, my friend the super will get it for you."

"You will come?"

"I'll be there," I said.

Damn right I would.

I hung up and reached for my coat. Before I could get it on, there was a single rap followed by two quick ones on the door, and when I opened it Hooker and James slid inside, checked around automatically, then Hooker said, "You're hot, Tiger. The cops are checking every hotel in the city and they're all after you."

"Why?"

"Two old dames in the Shrevesport got shook up about Ann being killed and described the guy who checked their registry cards. Just by accident the cop taking the report was the one you worked with when you were interrogating the guests. Then Ann's identity was made from prints in the New York file taken when she was doing nightclub work. An astute reporter remembered her from another case involving Martin Grady so the quick thinkers got to you."

"IATS come in on it?"

"That's what Newark Control told us to report to you. CIA has a team in the field and some more from the other branches. They haven't hit here yet so you clear out. We'll take care of the bill and all. Martin Grady called in personally and said you were to continue as instructed."

"Anything on Gabin Martrel?"

"He's still in City General."

"Okay and thanks. I'll call through Newark if I need you. The police have photos of me by now so I'll sit in a movie all day and move around after dark until I can get squared away. You stay on tap."

"Yes, sir. Watch your step."

Then I felt my lips split in a grin. I picked up the phone, dialed Thomas Watford's number and when I got him I said, "The kill in the Shrevesport Hotel, buddy . . . it's part of the Martrel thing. Ann Lighter was one of us, all right. She had picked up where Bill Copely left off and got caught at it by the same gang that's trying to dump your defector friend."

"What was she looking for, Mann?"

I laughed at him. "I'll do better than tell you. I'll show you someday soon." When I hung up, he was still swearing at me.

I picked a movie on Times Square and sat in it for ten hours. I made use of the time by getting some more sleep, but even then it was a long day. When I came out it was dark, and after I grabbed a quick sandwich I hopped a cab over to Ernie Bentley's lab.

He had been filled in on all the details to date, but like all technicians in this peculiar business, he was only interested in his own phase of it. He did what he was asked to . . . fitted me out with makeup and plastic that changed the shape of my face enough so nobody would be making me with a casual once-over. I dropped the suit, put on a tweed jacket and slacks that were aged enough to make them look right for the neighborhood I'd be in, then checked the action on the .45.

Ernie said, "Sorry to hear about Ann."

"Yeah."

"The police said it took a powerful pair of hands to do the job. She got it quick."

He looked at me, waiting for an answer. "She got suckered somehow," Ernie said. "I issued her an automatic when she took the assignment."

"You'll find it in my bag over there."

"Ann had plenty of experience . . ." he began.

"We all do, Ernie. All it takes is one mistake."

"So if the situation was kosher she would have had a chance. How did she get suckered?"

"I don't know yet," I told him. "I have an idea, but I'm not sure."

"The other woman?"

"Possibly."

Ernie went back into the room and returned a few seconds later with a small plastic tube. He jerked it apart and took out a black ball-point pen and held it in the palm of his hand. One of his pet hobbies was the development of ultrahigh explosive compounds, and he was continually working them into special equipment gadgets. "Like it?"

"Neat. What's it for?"

"Who knows? It looks like a pen and writes like one, but when you take off the protective cap, put it on the other end and give it a half-turn you have the equivalent of three sticks of dynamite with a one-minute-delayed fuse set. It might come in handy."

"Stable?"

"Better than what I gave you the last time. This isn't sensitive to shock or heat. It's an acid-reaction type and it has to be set deliberately." He handed it to me, his face serious. "If you use it, turn in a detailed report."

I took it from him, studied the piece a minute, then stuck it in my coat pocket. "I don't like carrying this junk."

His eyes roamed over my face. "The way you look you might need it. Right now you'd stand in for any prelim fighter."

I grunted at him, stuck the pen in my inside coat pocket and picked up the phone. On the second number I got the voice I wanted and told him to meet me at the Blue Ribbon Restaurant on Forty-fourth Street in twenty minutes and hung up.

During the war Charlie Corbinet had been the C.O. of our group, a full colonel who had spent a lifetime in espionage, winding up as head of one of the most top-secret operations in the ETO. When the big smash was over they upped him to a BG, but his policies, based on knowledge and firsthand experience, were too advanced for the do-gooders who were giving our country away and he was forced into retirement. But when they needed him again he was ready, and using his civilian occupation as a cover, he went into IATS to handle their tougher projects.

Oh, he knew about us, all right. In his own way he had helped out a few times when we were able to go inside a situation a government agency couldn't handle without exposing us to foreign-born hate propaganda. One thing he did understand that the others didn't . . . there was a need for people like us to help hold the Red tide in check.

We sat at the corner of the bar sipping a dark Pryor beer, and as quickly as I could I gave him a rundown on what had happened. When I told him about Sonia Dutko he said, "You picked up a detail we missed, Tiger. We knew about her, of course, but we didn't consider Martrel's defection to be linked with a dame."

"Why not?"

"His age, for one thing."

"Right now he's at a dangerous age. What else?"

"The position he held. He was right at the top. It doesn't seem logical that he would cut out after all that work."

"So for the love of a woman . . ." I said.

He grinned at me. "You ought to know."

"Okay, I almost made the same mistake. I was a lot younger."

"When do you marry Rondine?" He stopped, looked at me sharply. "Sorry, you have me doing it too. Edith Caine. I keep forgetting Rondine's dead. When I saw Edith I made the mistake you did . . . she's the spitting image of her older sister."

"When it's over. Maybe."

"Tough." He took a pull of his beer, put it down and made wet circles on the bar with the bottom of the glass. "What do you want from me?"

"Get inside the Shrevesport Hotel and check everybody out. Everybody. If the Dutko dame is clear, it means somebody else pulled the cork on Ann Lighter. It could have been the same one who took those shots at me outside. I can't see a woman making a kill like that. It took too damn much strength."

"She was a trained athlete. She must have had powerful hands and arms."

"Nuts. Women only come so strong. Can you arrange it?"

Charlie Corbinet stared into his glass a moment, nodded and said, "You got something else on your mind too, haven't you?"

"I didn't think it showed."

"It doesn't, Tiger ... it's just that I know you better than you think."

"Keep a tail on Rondine. If they're after me they might try to get to her too. There's nobody else I can ask but you, and you can pull the right strings if you want to."

"Rondine," he mused. "Yes, they might try something at that."

"Well?"

"Of course." He finished the beer, put the glass down and said, "Will I be hearing from you or will all your reports go to Martin Grady?"

"We'll be in touch," I said. I threw two bucks on the bar, tapped his shoulder so long and went back outside.

A cabbie dropped me three blocks away from where I wanted to go and I walked the rest of the way. Twice I passed uniformed cops and got nothing more than a casual glance. If you walked fast enough to look like you had a destination, if you were dressed a little over the hump that makes it doubtful you're on the bum and possibly employed, they let you go. With the right face and a lousy-looking mugging prospect, the punks lay off you and the hookers don't bother making a pitch.

When I reached the house, I went up the sandstone steps that had been hollowed by generations of feet and shoved the door open. I pushed the button marked *Super*, waited until Fat John came down the corridor and stood scowling up at me. "Whatta ya want?"

"It's what you want, buddy. Like Martin Grady's money." I said the next word that coded me in, and a smile turned his round face into a mass of creases.

"Geez ... you ain't ..."

"Same one as before."

He reached out, shut the door quickly and waved a thumb toward the stairs. "The broad's right up the top. She hasn't left the joint."

"Any trouble?"

"Nope. I done like you said."

"Who else is here?"

"Nobody. Just the broad and me. One of you guys from Chicago stayed two days before she come and left. He didn't say nothin' like always."

"Fine, John. Now keep the door locked while I'm here."

He reached out, turned the handle and threw a door chain on. "Sure, Tiger. I'll be down here if you want somethin'."

I nodded, let him walk back then edged over to the stairs. Up there could be the key to the whole operation. *Plato* could hinge on her and so could a lot of lives. I went up slowly, got to the door and tapped out the signal.

From behind the door her voice sounded tense. "Yes . . . who is it?"

"Tiger Mann."

"How . . . do I know?"

I took out the lethal pen Ernie Bentley had given me, wrote T. Mann on a scrap of paper and shoved it under the door. "Check the handwriting with the note you have."

Slowly, she drew the paper in, and after a few seconds the bolts slid back and it opened and there was Sonia Dutko.

Somehow, she wasn't at all what I had expected. Ashblonde hair framed a lovely oval face that was accentuated by high cheekbones and beautiful dark eyes that had an almost Oriental cast. Her mouth was full, nervously wet, and with each deep breath of controlled fear she took, her breasts swelled against a taut nylon blouse. There was no athletic dumpiness about her that the earlier pictures had showed. She was lithe, trim, her hips almost mannish but with thighs and calves that had all the grace of a dancer's.

"Don't let my looks fool you, honey," I said. "Good make-up job."

She let a smile touch her mouth and I knew her eyes found signs of Ernie's touch-up that would be missed by a man. "I . . . didn't know who to expect." Her voice was low, but still carried traces of an accent, though it would be difficult to tell of what variety.

I shut the door, checked the place out of habit, then pointed to a chair. When she sat down, I perched on the arm of the old couch opposite her and said, "You want to talk?"

"Don't you . . . think I must?"

"I do."

"Then I will talk."

"What happened at the hotel?"

"This woman . . . she came to me and said it was necessary that I leave. She said it was important to Gabin's safety. While she was there someone knocked on the door. She would not let me answer. A few minutes later the phone rang and I could not answer that either."

"Who knew you were here?"

"I . . . nobody. I told no one."

"Ann . . . the woman . . . know that?"

"Yes, I told her." She folded her hands tightly, licked her lips and looked back at me again.

Sonia said, "She was afraid they would come back so she gave me this paper where to go and made me leave quickly down the stairs. I went out the back way and she stayed there. I came right here."

"You contacted nobody?"

"Just you," she said. "Please . . . tell me, what happened?"

"They came for you, baby. Ann took it for you. She stayed to cover your exit and they nailed her."

"But how?"

"My guess is that she answered the door hoping to fool them with the wrong face and they saw through it. She could identify them from then on and they couldn't take the chance."

She covered her mouth with one hand and her eyes seemed to get hazy a moment. "Oh. That is . . . so terrible."

"Why did you come to New York, Sonia?"

"It was because of Gabin. When I heard what he did . . ."

"Defect?"

"Yes."

"Did he do it because of you?"

She shook her head, a puzzled expression crossing her face, then she understood. "No. I do not think that can be. Since . . . I left there we never wrote."

"You two had a big thing going at one time there, didn't you?"

"Yes, at one time. It was . . . the excitement of the games. Gabin was an important man then and it was nice. He was very gentle."

"Did he know you felt like that?"

"Who can tell how a man hopes? He was not young."

I shrugged, watching her. "Age hasn't that much to do with it. He was in love with you, wasn't he?"

Her head went down and she studied her hands again. She nodded slowly, her eyes wet. "Yes. I did not want it to be so."

"Tell me one thing. And answer straight. Did he help you escape?"

She couldn't have fooled me. I'd been around too long not to have seen it if she tried. Very simply, she said, "No, my Tiger, he did not. I left because I had enough. It was a sudden decision. When I saw the others . . . met other young people at the games and heard them talk and saw how they were I knew I had to leave. It was very easy. At home I had no one that could pay for my . . . defection. I merely took advantage of the situation and left. Some . . . friends lent me money. Your country was kind enough to do the rest and take me in. I have tried to be a good person here."

"You changed your name several times."

"Yes," she agreed. "Even here there are those who remember and who threaten. I have been . . . approached on occasions. Each time I would move away. I want no part of the past. It is a new life here."

"Then what did you want from Martrel?"

She moved her shoulders in a gesture of despair. "I knew what he would go through. I did not want him to be alone." She stopped, looked up with misty eyes. "There was a time when I thought perhaps . . . he did do it for me. I felt responsible. I wanted to be sure. But it cannot be for me. Since the games, we never even wrote. It would have been too dangerous for him to hear from me. It is very difficult to speak of this thing now."

"It'll be dangerous for you, too."

"But why?"

"Your former compatriots think they might be able to get to him through you. If they can nail you they can put the pressure on Martrel so he won't talk to our people. He could even be induced to return. They've already made one attempt on his life."

Her face registered the shock of my words. "Is he . . ."

"Okay. He's in the hospital under guard. He'll be all right, but they won't stop with just one try."

"Then I must see him. Oh, I must."

"In time, baby. Right now you're as important as he is."

"But what is it you want me to do?"

"Just stay under cover until I get to Martrel. Once he knows you're safe he'll talk. Once he's talked, his value to the Soviets will be nil and he won't be the same kind of target. He'll be finished as far as the homeland is concerned and he'll have a certain amount of safety over here."

"Certain amount!"

"You can't keep everybody away from his door, but with a new cover identity . . ."

"He said he wanted to teach and . . ."

"That part's up to him. Others have done it before. If he wants to take that chance it's his business. You know how they operate over there. They aren't about to let anybody off the hook if they can help it, but if by making a move against him when he's no longer of value it puts a crimp in their operations he's better off left alone. We're just going to have to sweat it out."

Sonia stood up suddenly, her entire body tight with anxiety. "But there must be something . . ."

I held my hand up for her to be quiet.

Outside the door there had been a sound that shouldn't have been there and I could feel it go through me right down to my toes.

I waved Sonia over to a corner, motioned for her to get down on the floor and when she was curled up there, toed over and flipped off the light. I yanked the .45 out, pulled the hammer back off half cock so it was ready and looked down at the crack under the door.

The faint hall light should have shone in, but it wasn't there now. Someone had turned it out so there wouldn't be any shadows coming through and if they needed the darkness for cover they would have it.

I had spotted the radio when I came in the room, a small, old plastic affair and I felt for it, switched it on and when the tubes warmed up, found a station with soft music and turned it to a level barely loud enough to cover any sounds we might make. If the company outside hadn't identified me they might take my visit for a romantic one and try to wait me out before pulling a break-in.

"Sonia . . ." I whispered.

"Yes?" I could barely hear her voice.

"We're going out the window up to the roof. Think you can make it?"

"Whatever . . . you say. Are they . . ."

"Don't talk. Come on." I held out my hand, felt hers find mine and pulled her to her feet. The music stopped then and so did we. For thirty seconds an announcer spieled on and we stood there motionless; then when the music started again, we went across the room to the window.

Fat John had kept things well oiled. The window went up noiselessly and we both stepped out on the rusted steel platform. I pointed upward, and Sonia nodded and reached for the rungs of the ladder-type fire escape. Then I closed the window and followed her. Above my head I could see the white flash of her thighs as she climbed effortlessly, swaying with the loose swing of a professional athlete.

At the third floor I stopped her. "Go on up and wait there. Stay behind a parapet or a chimney and stay in the shadows.

Keep your head down and don't move unless you know it's me."

"Yes, Tiger."

The window beside me was locked, but I took out the roll of adhesive tape from my pocket, crisscrossed the glass several times, held my elbow against the pane, then with one sharp slap of my hand against my fist, knocked it out without a sound. I reached in, unlatched it, swung it open and climbed inside.

I used a match to spot the furniture, located it and went across to the door and pulled it open. For a full three minutes I stood there, my ears deciphering the sounds that filtered into the house. Then I heard the slight whisper of one breathing. A minute later I knew there were two of them.

Both were standing below me, flanking the door, and they weren't going to be standing there long.

I took out the book of matches, ripped one off and put the cover behind the rest so that they were all exposed. Then I closed my eyes, struck the one in my hand, flamed the entire book at once and threw it over the rail.

They had heard the match strike but they weren't ready for the entire book. In that total darkness it lit the place up like a flare and I had one chance to spot them as they turned with startled shouts and raised the guns. They couldn't see me behind the light and my eyes were dark adjusted and besides the two quick spurts of flame from the .45 the last thing they ever saw was that tiny sunlight burst coming down over their heads. I got one in the neck and the other in the chest, and they smashed into the wall with final choking noises, and in a few seconds lay there still.

I didn't wait. I went down the stairs to the first floor and back to Fat John's room, yanked the hall light so that it threw a feeble yellow glow throughout the place and when I saw his door standing open I knew what I was going to find.

Fat John wasn't going to collect anymore Martin Grady paychecks. He lay in a puddle of his own blood with his throat slit up from one end to the other.

Outside somebody had already started to shout and across the street I saw the lights of a car blossom on and watched it pull away from the curb. There wasn't much time. I raced back to the landing, checked the bodies for identification and found nothing, then went upstairs to the roof. I shoved the door open, called, "Sonia . . . it's me, Tiger."

"Over here." Her voice came from my left and I stepped out

so she could see me, kicking the door shut with my foot.

Already two sirens were screaming our way from opposite directions. She came to me then, frightened and trembling. I held her hand, scrambled over one roof after another until we reached the end of the block, then located a fire escape and felt our way down. When we reached the street I hooked my arm under hers and walked away as if nothing had ever happened.

When we were far enough off, I flagged down a cab, gave the driver Ernie Bentley's address, got off at the corner and paid the driver. As he handed me the change, a bulletin was coming in on his radio about the three murders in the neighborhood we had just left.

We sat in the back office of the lab while Ernie Bent- **6**
ley went through channels to get anything new on the
killings. So far the cops were at a loss, but they had
established entry through a back window, and the knife that
chopped down Fat John was still in one of the dead men's
pockets. No identification had been found on the bodies so the
police were putting their prints through the usual processing.
Several witnesses had seen a late model dark sedan leave the
scene immediately after the shootings, but nobody had picked
up the make or license number.

The first thing Ernie had done was throw a new barrel into
the .45 and rework the pin so I wasn't worried about a
ballistics check pinning my rod into it. What they had in their
files was already obsolete because the gun had been worked
over since the last ballistics photos were taken. In case I was
picked up and a paraffin test made on my hand, Ernie used a
solvent to wipe out all traces of nitrate. He was worried about
the matchbook I had used until I assured him it was of a
common variety and not traceable. It would have burned up
and no prints were going to come off it.

But what got me was Sonia. She had left tracks all around
the place, and with her prints in the Washington file she was
going to be on the wanted list in a matter of hours.

When Ernie came back his face was tight and he said,
"How'd they get to Fat John's?"

I looked at Sonia. "Go over it again, kid . . . how you left
the hotel."

She gave us the story in detail for the third time.

"You sure nobody followed you?"

"There was no one I saw," she told us.

"Hell," Ernie said, "she's no pro. How could she tell if someone was there or not? They wouldn't be stupid enough to try a hit like that alone. They probably had the exits covered in case something like this happened."

"That's what I'm thinking. When she got to the street it was too crowded to pull anything, so a tail followed her to John's and they moved in at their own convenience. My being there slowed down the action just a little bit."

Ernie nodded, then walked over beside Sonia and said suddenly, "Hold out your hands."

Not understanding, she did as he told her to. Ernie took both of them in his and scrutinized them carefully, pushing her sleeves back to expose her forearms. There was nothing rough textured about them. They were delicate, smooth and obviously not those of a strenuously trained athlete any longer. Years ago she had given it up to become a woman. Very carefully he felt the line of her muscles and the backs and edges of her hands and I knew what he was looking for.

When he finished I said, "Well?"

"She didn't do it."

It came to her then, slowly, then she set her mouth and gave each one of us a direct look. "No, my friends, it was not I who killed that girl."

"No sweat, honey," I said. "In this business you have to be sure or you get dead in a hurry. Right now the cops are going in circles trying to track you down and if they find you there will be some tall explanations. As far as I am concerned, I'll stick with Ernie's decision and my own opinions. I saw what happened to Ann Lighter. I had seen other kills just like it, sugar, and it takes a powerful set of hands to do that."

She still was direct and somehow aloof. "Perhaps I could have used a weapon."

I didn't take the bait. "Uh-uh. That was inflicted manually."

"Then thank you for that," she said.

Ernie let go her hands and turned back to me. "What are you going to do with her?"

I shrugged. "She's out of clothes and has no place to stay. She's got to be with somebody we can trust."

"Get somebody over from Newark Control."

"No time. There's a team out after Martrel and her, and they know she's still with me. The only safe bet is grabbing the bunch they assigned to knock them off. If we can hold up their action until Martrel talks we can take the heat off both of them. Look . . . I want you to do something."

"What?"

"Get a photo of Sonia and me together. We'll use today's paper as a date identification. If Martrel knows she's okay maybe we can break him loose."

"Come on inside," Ernie said.

It only took a few minutes to get the photo taken, and while we waited for the print to dry I got Charlie Corbinet on the phone. I laid it out for him in detail and told him to try to get a make on the dead men through the foreign agent file. He let out a slow whistle when he heard the news, but knew better than suggest I lay off and didn't bother asking any questions. He'd get the information as it came, but right now I was ahead of the game and was going to stay that way.

I said, "Anything on the Shrevesport Hotel job?"

"A few interesting facts. One . . . no men were seen entering the place and none of the fire doors that were locked from the outside showed any signs of forcible entry. Two . . . the women at the desk saw at least a dozen people take the elevators upstairs, but aside from two, they didn't know whom they were visiting, and all those people were females. It still looks like a man's job, but a good, hefty broad well trained in the science of murder could have done it just as well. A few of those females fitted the type."

"I don't like it, Colonel."

"Neither do I, but that's all we have to go on."

"You have a tail on Rondine yet?"

"Right after your call Albert Cutter was assigned to her. Not so much to keep an eye on her, but to watch out for you. Be careful of that boy, Tiger. He doesn't think much of your operation."

"Nobody does."

"But not like him. Since Martin Grady got that Senate Investigation floundering he'd like to put the hook in you people. I have an idea he's on a double assignment."

"Thanks. But why the info?"

"Because in a way I have a feeling for what you're doing. I was there too, remember? This country is still run by the civilian factor even if it intrudes on governmental domain. There are some aspects of our security policies I've never favored and when something has to be done it has to be done by pros regardless of whose toes get stepped on."

"How high up has it gone?"

"At present Gabin Martrel is this country's choicest morsel in the feast of self-preservation."

"So?"

"I can't tell you any more than that, Tiger boy."

"Stow it. So it's in a committee now. All the agencies are on it."

"And you're the target," he said. "You're a hunted man."

" 'Twas ever thus, buddy."

"You'll have to come out real clean on this one."

"Balls," I told him, then said so long and hung up.

Ernie looked at me carefully, nodded for me to come over to the side of the room. "How far you going with her?"

"All the way, kid. She's the key."

"And tonight?"

"I take her back to the hotel. It's a fleabag and a ten-spot to the clerk can get Mata Hari into my room."

He glanced at my face. "They won't know you at the desk like that."

"Then let's dump the junk. One way or another my face is chalked in. The driver of that car might have spotted me and I'd only have to change the mask anyway."

"Sit down. I'll get the solvents. Some of it might hurt to get off."

"Great," I said.

While he took off the plastic and the makeup, Sonia sat to one side in absolute fascination. She watched while he peeled off the garbage and put me back where I belonged. Once more the nose and chin were my own, the long sloppy hair turned into a tight crew chop and my teeth stopped bulging past my lips. I got rid of the clothes, climbed back into my own fitted suit that could hide the fat .45 so nicely, stuck the crazy ball-point pen that was charged to the hilt in my pocket, picked up my money and got out of the chair.

For the first time she laughed and it sounded good. Her voice had a funny, low quality of genuine pleasure that put a glow on her face, and her deep, dark eyes were full of sparkle.

"Good joke," I said. I just didn't like anybody laughing at me.

"No, my Tiger, no joke. Before you seemed so like a . . . a . . ."

"Bum," I finished.

"Yes. But now you are different. I can see the tiger now. I can see why you are called the Tiger."

"Not *the*, honey. Just Tiger. It's my real name."

"You deserve it. But it seems you need a long tail."

I gave her a dirty grin, and for a second she stopped laughing, then she smiled again. "I understand," she said seriously.

"Brother," Ernie laughed, "do you fieldmen have all the luck."

"Drop dead," I said. I took Sonia's hand and she came off the stool. "Let's go."

It only took a five-spot to the clerk and no questions asked. He never even bothered to look up, but pocketed the bill and went back to his paper. It was an old story and he wasn't interested in other people's troubles.

The thread check on the door was still secure so I left the rod in my rig and went on in. When I turned the key in the lock, she stood with her back to the wall, her eyes gauging me carefully. There was one chair, one dresser and one bed and it wasn't a very big bed at that.

"Tiger . . . ?"

I gave it to her straight down the line. "Baby, you're standing on top of three dead people and the fourth could be me, you or Martrel. You might not like the operation but you're not asking and I'm not answering. I've thrown away more broads than most guys ever get and this isn't the time to play footsies. I didn't bring you here to slap you in the sack. If I wanted to I'd do it and you wouldn't even let out a bawl. When it was done you'd cry with pleasure, but to get the idea out of your mind, you wait until you're asked before you say no. Keep that in your head, kiddo. This isn't a game we're playing and as far as I'm concerned, I'll belt you into sleepy-land with one shot in the jaw if that's what it takes to quiet you down."

"I've never . . ."

"You a virgin?"

She gave me a long, quiet look then, her eyes telling me nothing. Finally she said, "No."

"This is just a stopover until I can get you under cover." I walked to the phone, gave the operator Rondine's number *. . . damn, I couldn't stop calling her that! Rondine was dead and this was her sister, Edith Caine. Edith Caine! But the name was too long in my mind and I couldn't get it out. Edith was the real Rondine. The Rondine that Rondine should have been.*

The phone rang and rang and nobody answered, so I hung

up. I looked at my watch. It was late. Very late. Too damn late.

I said, "Take the bed. I'll sleep in the chair."

She nodded just once, walked over and sat on the edge of the bed. I knew she was watching me when I slumped in the chair with my feet on the windowsill, but I was at that point where I didn't give a flying hoot anymore. You don't look at a dead friend and then kill two persons yourself without something happening inside and it had been a long day. Outside they were hunting both of us by now. We were the targets and the shooters were people on both teams, and unless we were careful we'd be caught in the crossfire. Right and Might. Which was the answer? You had to have both to win. I stared out across the tops of the buildings into the soft glow that was New York at night, watching the color of the city change with the flash of the neon signs and listening to it cry down on the streets below and wondered where else people were dying and for what cause.

I fell asleep with the .45 cradled in my hand, and like rain in the distance I heard the shower splashing the soft, throaty humming of some old song I remembered from Europe long ago and smelled the fragrance of soap and softness of a woman.

Her hands were gentle as they touched my face and woke me, fingers tracing lines up the sides of my cheeks to my eyes, then stroking my hair with the flat of palms that had an urgency all their own, yet moved quietly so they could give pleasure without asking any in return.

Outside the window the sun was coming up in a glazed, orange arc that filtered through the haze and I reached up and felt her hands under my own.

"Tiger," she said. "My Tiger . . . come sleep with me."

It was a beautiful sunrise, slow and easy at first, then with crashing suddenness the wild red and bright burst in upon both of us in a frenzy of delight, then diminished into the steadily increasing glow of morning.

Damn, how soft she was, how firm and round the fleshy curves and hollows. Right from the fierce steppes of a Caucasus mountain she brought every buck, every undulation into a living symphony of outlandish delight. Her mouth was a hot, wet thing of such demanding passion that it itself was a fuse that ignited one explosion after another. Her mouth melted against mine, a torch that could nearly scream unless it was choked off, her entire body an octopus of emotion that demanded and demanded and when it was satisfied for a short time was almost content in a relaxation close to death itself.

But I wouldn't give her that relaxation. She asked, now she got. She wanted to see what a tiger was like and now she had to find out. She knew the depth of the canines and the feeling of being absorbed because she was only a woman in the lust of a horrible hunger and in that frightening sunlight she knew for the first time what it was like to live as one.

Later the shadows came as the sun went overhead and into the west. Later I ran the shower, dressed and woke her, and while she was still perfumed with the sweet smell of sleep, I hated the hell out of myself while I looked into her eyes and said, "Up, baby. Rise and shine."

Across the space of two feet my .45 was lying there at full cock ready to kill somebody.

And now I had to call Rondine.

How do you cover a wedding night shot to bits and the night after and the night after? How do you keep the cold out of your voice or the thing you feel?

She picked up the phone after it had rung twice and said hello. I tried to keep my voice where it belonged. "Tiger, honey."

"Oh?"

"I need you, kitten. Can you help?"

"Tiger . . . you really don't need anybody at all."

"I need you now."

"Please, Tiger."

"Oh, goddamn it, shut up and listen. You want to act like a stupid broad then go ahead. I'm so sick and tired of the crap women throw out I want to spit. So stuff it, kid. I don't ask again. Sorry I loused up your wedding, but some things come first and this is one. You come second and if you ever get a man you'll always come second to the job, so drop dead. You . . ."

She didn't let me finish at all. "Tiger . . . can I say I'm sorry?"

"Sure, doll, but it may not count. This isn't the same deal. It's like the last time when everybody's ass was on the hook."

"I know."

"Pig's tail you don't. We already have three dead people at our feet and try being dead once." I grabbed the .45 in a cold sweat and shoved it in my belt just to keep my hand from shaking.

I heard her sharp intake of breath and the catch in her

voice when she said, "Whatever you want, I'll do, darling." She had the touch of London in her words, a little more thickly than usual.

Hell, what did I expect? I was getting better than I deserved anyway. "You working today?"

She was a translator at the UN, but had a tie with the British Embassy with prior training in England that could fit her for a lot of things. Things she never mentioned, but I knew about. In off-hours from her regular job she was inside top-secret meetings of their staff and when necessity demanded it, acted as courier or agent for their select personnel.

"I'll be at the General Assembly until eleven. After that I have some private paperwork to do. Nothing that can't wait, however."

"Good. Now listen and don't ask questions. You have a tail on you, a CIA man named Albert Cutter." I gave her a rapid description of the guy then, and added, "He's there for your protection and to get a lead on me. Right now I'm hot. When you get to your office, have your boys spot him. If you can't, then cut out and get over here to the Bristol End, that little fish place I took you to once."

"I remember it."

"Bring along a suitcase of clothes. . ." I looked at Sonia and measured her absently . . . "size twelve, and include dark glasses, a raincoat, hat . . . anything that can disguise a woman. I'll meet you there at noon."

"Very well."

"Okay, baby."

"And Tiger . . ."

"What?"

"I love you. Sometimes . . . you mix me up, but I do understand."

"Then where the hell do you go at night?" I asked her, not able to keep the annoyance out of my voice.

Rondine laughed lightly, the way a woman does when she has you hanging. "Wouldn't you like to know?" she said.

Sonia was smiling too, but only with her eyes, smiling with the knowledge of last night and this morning and the triumph of one woman over another woman when a man was the prize.

"This one you call," she asked, "she is your girl?"

"We were going to be married until this came up."

"Ah, I am sorry, but now I can understand your passion." Her full, luscious mouth curved in a gentle laugh. "And I think you can understand mine. It is no good when you are too long without someone."

"Yeah."

"She will never know, Tiger."

"Let's hope not."

"You regret?"

I got up, walked over to her and held her face in my hands. She was beautiful standing there in the full light of the sun, her ash-blonde hair gone almost white. "No, doll, no regrets. It was lovely and necessary. You're very much a woman."

She raised herself, kissed me lightly, drew back a moment to study my face then came back into my arms again in a new burst of sunrise, cushioning herself against me so that every curve of her body fitted mine. I felt her fingers digging into my back and her tongue was a probing thing searching for answers, and when I finally held her away she said, "I hope ... it's not over, my Tiger."

I tilted her chin up with my finger. "Let's not press our luck."

At ten o'clock I went down to the lobby and called the Colonel from a coin booth. He was right on tap, asked somebody to leave his office and said, "You clear?"

"Roger."

"Then let me give it to you fast. The CIA got a make on one of those two dead men you left behind. Identification came through Mexico City. He was picked up after the kill but broke out and apparently came into the U.S. on another assignment. Interpol has a line on him and he's a gun hand with a fat past. So far nothing on the other one except his shoes. They're foreign made. No photos or prints on file here but they're sending copies to our people overseas."

"Somebody here is giving them orders."

"Certainly. We can pinpoint the head of the operation but can't break their channel of communication to get at the cell they're using. They'll have all specialists on this project and don't want anything cutting back to them if it falls through."

"What about Sonia Dutko?"

"A quiet A.P.B. from the locals. IATS put the squash on it, but it's there. Meanwhile all the agencies have been notified and the teams are working it out. How long are you going to hold her?"

"Long enough to get the job done. Any way you can get them off my own neck?"

"Not a chance, Tiger, not a chance. Because of our past

relationship they're watching me to check any communication with you."

"They think you're feeding me?"

"Could be a guess there. I'll probably have somebody on my phone from now on."

"Then leave any messages with George at the Blue Ribbon or check in with Wally Gibbons. I'll pick them up there."

"Right. Stay out of trouble."

"Yeah, sure."

At noon I left the hotel with Sonia on my arm, took a chance that we wouldn't be spotted and grabbed a cab over to the Bristol End. It was a small fish and chips place a wily Londoner opened on the West Side and drew a lot of trade from the freighter crews. Rondine had gotten hungry for the stuff one night and Wally Gibbons told me about it. For a reporter, the next best thing to news was something for his stomach.

Only a few were at the counter so far. I pointed to the corner table in the back, ordered three plates and some beer and sat down facing the door. I knew I was edgy, but didn't realize to what extent until Rondine walked in, then I was on my feet going to meet her while both the counterman and his customers gave approving glances to something they rarely got to see. One said in a half whisper, "He even got two. Some guys got all the luck."

I introduced the two women, let them sit together with me opposite them and gave Rondine a picture of events as quickly as possible. When I brought her up to date, I said, "I want her out of town . . . someplace where she can stay without being seen until I can get to Martrel."

Rondine nodded. "Remember Burton Selwick?"

"How could I forget?"

"He won't be back from his leave for another month. Before he went to England he said I could use his summer place in Connecticut whenever I wanted. It's only a little over an hour away and I have the keys."

"Have you been there?"

"Several times. It should be ideal. It would only take a day to have the utilities hooked up, and the place is well stocked with food."

"Okay, we'll use it." I pulled some bills out of my pocket and handed them to Rondine. "Rent a car, get her up there and come right back. If there's anything you need, get it on the way because I don't want Sonia leaving the house at all. Understood?"

Sonia said, "It will be safe?"

"As good as any. If our people pick you up, you can still be a target for a 'scoped rifle. I've even seen them wipe out four people with a grenade just to get the one they wanted. No, I don't want you picked up just yet. You sit in that house until I contact you . . . or Rondine does. Nobody else."

"But Gabin . . ."

"I'll get to him, don't worry."

When we finished lunch the girls went to the washroom with the suitcase and Sonia Dutko had a change of costume when she came back. The hat was a trick one that effectively hid her face and the way she had her hair swept down made her high cheekbones unnoticeable. With the glasses on she wasn't going to be easy to spot.

I paid the bill, told Rondine to meet me at the Blue Ribbon at six, hustled them into a cab and walked the opposite way toward the dock area to catch a cruising cab rather than head up toward the main stem where there would be cops with my picture fresh on their minds.

On the corner I picked up a paper, went through the headlines and the news report that had the triple killings in big, bold type. Although it was a sensational affair, nothing had leaked out to the press about the true nature of the thing so I knew how tight Washington had clamped the lid down.

I folded the paper under my arm, checked for a cab and when I saw none, walked south hoping to catch one coming across town. Three blocks farther on I still hadn't seen an empty, but I did see a squad car easing down the street, and to ease the odds of being seen, casually started across the street toward the pier.

The ship that was in the last stages of being loaded there was the *Maitland*. Clement Fletcher's ship, the guy who blew his wad on a Geiger counter he never got to use. I wondered who the hell had swiped it on him. The hock-shop value wouldn't go over fifty bucks, and it was a lousy way to push a guy over the edge.

I used the press card to get past the gate, found the dock foreman and asked him if any of the crew were around.

"You want a job, try the union hall. These guys can't do you any good."

"No job," I told him. "A little information, that's all."

"Then go on up. They're probably playing cards for

matches on the other side in the sun. They always come back early when they run out of dough."

I went up the gangplank, worked my way across the deck cargo until I heard voices and the slap of cards going down. There were only two of them there, looking like they had been through the mill. Both needed shaves and seemed in the middle of a hangover. Instead of money they were playing for paper matches torn out of a few books, and they never even bothered to look up at me until I dropped a ten-spot in front of each one.

Then they looked up all right.

One guy fingered the bill and said, "So what's it for?"

"Talk."

They looked at each other, nodded and the same one said, "So long as you don't ask us to mail no letters overseas or carry somethin' to a friend. That crap is out."

"Suits me."

"So talk then."

I sat on the edge of a hatch cover and shoved my hat back. "I had a friend in the crew. Clement Fletcher."

"Sure, the looney," the other one said. "Got tanked and fell in the river. He did the same thing in Brussels only got fished out in time. He could fall off a sidewalk, that guy."

"You remember him having a Geiger counter?"

Both of them nodded at once. "Drove us nuts with that thing. Always talking about making a big strike in S.A. somewhere."

"Perdes."

"Yeah, that's it. Why?"

"It was stolen from him."

The one guy shrugged and grinned a little. "So what? He can't use it where he is."

"The point is, buddy, I'd like to know who swiped it."

He looked at me, stretched and said, "Tell you something, so would I. It's no good when somebody gets in the crew's lockers. Never saw a trip yet where somebody didn't have a heavy hand. Once in a while he gets caught and there's fun below decks and the guy don't do it no more."

"This didn't happen at sea. The ship was docked right here."

"Ah, same thing. Once we get in people swarm all over the ship. This time the T-men come looking for dope that's supposed to be on board. They shake the ship down and don't find nothing. Hell, we coulda told 'em that. You think we don't know when a connection is made? Let me tell you somethin', mister. Me, I know about them things, the captain gets a report in a hurry. I got a young brother down in the hospital in Kentucky who was hooked while he was in high school. I hear about H on board and ..."

"Who else was here?"

"The usual. Guys from the front office. Longshoremen. Crew from the shipyard making minor repairs. All legit. We know 'em, right?"

The other guy nodded and picked up his cards. "Old Fletch talked too much about sinking all that dough into that machine. His whole roll. So it gets walked off the ship into a hock shop. I had a damn good watch go like that."

"Nobody else was here then?"

"Not till Fletch got drowned. Then a reporter come with the cops. Steve Mango had to go down and identify him. Lousy break. He owed me ten bucks."

I pointed to the bill in front of him. "Well, you just got it back."

There were fourteen hock shops in the general area that I picked out of the phone book. I went from one to the other looking to see if they had any Geiger counters in stock but all I got was a negative. What I was looking for was a handwriting sample of whoever checked it in, but it looked like they were smart enough to dump it in a shop someplace else in town. Covering every spot would be a major job single-handed so after the last place on my list I gave it up.

But there was still something scratchy about the whole deal that wasn't coming through to me. I couldn't afford the time or the chance of being picked up by processing something that wouldn't do Fletcher any good anyway, so I kissed off the *Maitland*, hopped a cab and went to the Blue Ribbon. It was almost six o'clock and I wanted to be sure to catch Rondine when she got in.

The supper crowd was already there so I told the waiter to get me in a back room and went into the phone booth. There was one curious angle to Fletcher's death that had just come to me and I had to put it through. If he had been poking around the ship with that crazy Geiger counter he might have stumbled on something else ... or somebody had thought he did. It wouldn't take much to murder a drunk. All you had to do was toss him in the drink.

I dialed Wally Gibbons and said, "Tiger here, buddy."

"Oh brother, here we go again."

"Look . . . use the power of the press and find something out for me, will you?"

"Do I get shot at?"

"Nothing like that."

"Tiger . . . if you're involved," he started, then: "Hell, everybody's looking for you. Damn, I'm getting bugged again."

"Relax. You never heard from me. This is something you might get a story out of."

"Well . . ."

"Call the Treasury Department office here and see if they came up with anything when they inspected the *Maitland.*"

His voice got serious then. "Narcotics?"

"Could be. See if they were tipped off. They might have found the junk and maybe not. Those guys don't act on hunches."

"I got it."

"A suspected accidental drowning of a man named Clement Fletcher from the same ship might turn into murder if the T-boys have anything. Look into it."

"Sure thing. Just as long as you're not involved."

"I'm not. It's just something I picked up along the way." I hung up, told Angie that Rondine was coming in and went back to the booth.

She was there at six and someplace along the line she had changed into a powder blue dress with a neckline that plunged deeply into the clefts of breasts so firm and beautiful it gave you a giddy feeling to look at her. When she threw off the coat she smiled, catching the travel of my eyes, and stood there until I swept them over her in pure appreciation.

"Sorry now?" she asked me in that teasing way she had sometime.

"Very." I pulled the chair back for her, sat so I could see whoever came past the booth and ordered a drink for us both. When it came I raised the glass in a silent toast, remembering the time we had both sat there and I was planning to kill her. Just to think of almost having done it made my fingertips turn cold.

We went through supper, let the rest of the crowd drift out, had one more drink and then I took the photo of me and Sonia Dutko out of my pocket and handed it to her. It was a close shot showing us both holding the three star edition of *The News* for date reference, and Rondine studied it closely.

"What shall I do with it?"

"Somehow you're going to get to Gabin Martrel at City

General Hospital. Give him that photo and tell him that she's safe. He can talk freely without putting her on the spot and when he's done it he can go right to her. I'm afraid the guy's in for a shock when he finds out she's a friend rather than being in love with him, but that's a personal affair he'll have to settle on his own."

"And him?"

"So he's in love. Frankly, I don't give a damn. We have to loosen his tongue and he won't talk until he's certain it won't kick back on her. Think you can do it?"

Very casually she dropped the photo in her bag. "I think so. Do you have any suggestions?"

"It's up to you now, kitten. Will do?"

"Will do," she said.

"Don't forget that tail. He'll want to see you come out of the same place you came in."

"I can arrange that."

"You know what I'd like to arrange?"

She smiled at me, slow and easy, a deliberate smile that had all the meaning in the world. "You're going to have to wait, darling. You stood me up, so now it's your turn to wait."

I didn't like the dig. I said, "Don't let me wait too long."

"Just long enough," she said.

I watched her leave, picked up the check when I finished my drink and paid it at the counter. When Angie gave me my change I said, "Damn," but he didn't know what I meant at all.

I went outside, turned toward Broadway and lost myself **7**
in the obscurity of the movie crowds that filled the
street. I turned south and just started walking, staying
with pedestrian traffic as if I had someplace to go, skirting the
occasional uniformed cops that seemed to mark every corner
of the Times Square area.

Three dead that we know of, I kept thinking; *how many
more to come?* The presence of one guy like Gabin Martrel
could disrupt the workings of two governments, putting one at
a disadvantage, the other on top. But as long as it was us in
the catbird seat I didn't give a damn.

OONA-3 that Martrel headed was their new close complex
spy system the Soviets had inaugurated even before World
War II had started. The people were placed, let grow to
fruition in strategic positions in other countries' politics and
economies and even surpassed the KGB. When they gave
Martrel the *Beltov Missile Project* because they thought he was
top security, they gave him a chance to use a mind that could
set them back five years in the race for dominance if he
decided to turn it over to us.

But would he do it?

If his defection was because of the woman and he could be
sure she was safe, he might. If his defection was based on
political disgust or the fact that his eyes were finally opened he
might not want any further involvement and simply would
take political asylum and let it go at that.

Until they bumped him. They weren't about to let a guy
with all that in his head run loose very long and he should

know it. Hell, maybe he didn't care anymore. That had happened before too.

My bet was that it all hinged on Sonia Dutko.

What would happen when the poor slob found out that it wasn't true love was anybody's guess, but that was his worry, not mine. The Soviets had a team ready to hit both of them. Me too. It would be a select group with fingers into everything and a head operator working directly under the Moscow office, kept in reserve especially for such an eventuality. Knock off the cell and you broke the chain. You had the time element you needed before a new one could get into operation.

What I'd like to know is how they got into the Shrevesport Hotel. IATS would have landed on that place like a swarm of ants, covering every angle. So what did they come up with? Nothing but women in the place, and the hit on Ann Lighter was undoubtedly made by a man.

And then I felt like a first-class jerk because the answer was so obvious.

I kept heading south, past the theater district, past the garment center and turned over to the block where the Shrevesport Hotel thrust its marquee out over the sidewalk. From across the street I cased the place as best I could, trying to spot anybody left from the investigating agencies. If they weren't outside, they'd be spotted in the lobby or on the floors. As far as I could tell, the exterior was clean.

The building extended backward into the next block and I approached it from there. On each side there was an alley with a series of fire escapes leading to the ground. Two metal doors faced me, locked on the outside, exits from the stairwells.

In a small cluster in both alleys were large green garbage cans, filled with the day's refuse from the hotel, every one filled to the brim. If this was typical of every day's collection, then it would have been like that when Ann was killed. There wasn't an inch of space to jam anything in them and with a killer looking for plenty of time to cover his tracks it would have had to be someplace else.

Each building flanking the hotel was as old and decrepit as the hotel itself, leftovers from a half century ago. They had basements whose windows were below pavement level with the small wells around them covered with rusted iron gratings. I checked every one of them on the east side, found nothing, then moved around to the west side.

In the second one I hit pay dirt. The grating had been lifted

up and stuffed down the well was a woman's dress, coat and a
wig, the dress well padded to bring a man's form up to
matronly size. A couple of sheets of newspaper jammed on top
of the clothing hid it well enough and made it look like just
another accumulation of junk that is common to all these old
places.

*So it was a man after all. And he had no trouble getting in
a hotel for women because he went in looking like one.*

I didn't want to cart the stuff around under my arm, so I
pushed it back in the well, went out to the street and walked
back to Broadway. At the first phone booth I called the
Colonel at his apartment and told him what I had found.

He said, "I think Hal Randolph is going to be glad to hear
this. He's been raising hell about you and Washington is on
his neck. They'd like to tear Martin Grady's operation to bits
but can't find a starting point. They thought they had it in
you."

"Just make sure they know where the credit goes."

"They might come up with an idea that isn't very pleasant."

I knew what he was getting at. "Like I planted the stuff?"

"That or using it yourself to make the hit."

"You know better than that."

"Still, they'll use any dodge to get to you, Tiger boy."

"Maybe. Get it covered. They ought to run down some lead
where the stuff was bought."

"Right away."

With another dime I bought a line into Dave Severn's office
and told him about the cache by the hotel. "Get over here fast,
Dave. If you're on tap when they find the stuff they won't try
anything funny. You can make it as quickly as they can and if
it ever comes up you can lead with your chin and leak it out
that I handed you the scoop."

"Will do, Tiger. You got any other items you want to give
away?"

"Plenty, but it isn't time."

"How about the Dutko babe?"

"That's what I have to hold."

"Oh man," he said. "You're up to your neck, aren't you?"

"And the water's hot," I told him. "Listen, for right now, if
they question you about being on the site, tell them you were
doing a follow-up piece for the paper."

"I know how to handle it."

"Good. I'll keep in touch. Don't write my obit yet."

"I did that a long time ago."

"So did a lot of other people. Most of them are dead now."

I picked up the eleven o'clock news on TV in a barroom just off Eighth Avenue. The announcer had the item last, but it was a spicy bit and they showed closeup stills of unidentified agents recovering the clothes the suspected murderer wore. The wig was a cheap one, an innocuous brown, the dress a blue print, the coat nondescript and the shoes flat-heeled and worn. None of the pieces had markings that could be immediately identified, but the police were tracing the sources and hopeful of an immediate arrest. As usual.

Police? There wouldn't have been a city cop in on the dodge unless he was specially assigned. This investigation was taking orders from Washington. With enough men and all the lab work they'd come up with something, but the other side was thinking on their feet too and those clothes were going to lead nowhere. All it did was give the police an M.O. possibility.

The last note the announcer came up with was that both women clerks in the hotel distinctly remembered a person dressed in the clothes going through the lobby, bypassing the desk and taking the elevator directly upstairs. The elevator operator partially corroborated the identification but couldn't recall what floor the person got off on. Most likely it wasn't the floor Ann was killed on, but another, then he walked back to the right one.

At eleven-thirty I eased back to my hotel and asked for my key. The night clerk reached for it absently, handed me a folded note and went back to the late sports news in his paper.

The simple message to call Mr. Donovan was a code that London wanted to contact me badly. It was about time Central had processed my reports and gotten some of the staff on it.

I called Newark from the pay station, spoke briefly to Virgil Adams and gave him my number, then let him call London to have them call me back. The overseas connection took fifteen minutes to make, and then I had Johnson on the other end and identified myself.

He was crisp and quick about it. "Have a message from behind the Iron Curtain, old boy. Ever hear of Spaad Helo?"

"Just heard of him, that's all. Headed up the Soviet interior purges, ran the operation that got the British atomic secrets, was suspected of killing our men in Buenos Aires and all that."

"It was Spaad, all right. Now you have him, we think. He was traced to Mexico and the trail was lost there, but our people think he skipped directly into the States on orders from Moscow. We do know his assignment is top priority and right now no better target exists than Gabin Martrel. They're in a tizzy over there trying to reorganize in case he spills the beans."

"Any photos or identification?"

"Not a thing. He's another of their mystery men. No face at all. Kept well in the shadows and all that. I doubt if more than a handful of people know his true identity. We'll see what we can get on him, but I'm afraid it won't be much. He speaks several languages and can handle American as well as you can, so be on your toes."

"You're not much help."

"One thing you might consider. Remember Sonny Carter ... you worked with him."

"Sure."

"He sent a memo in that during the atomic affair here when he was with British Intelligence, he hit a man during the gunfight. He thinks he caught him in the upper right arm and the man may have been Spaad."

"That's something anyway. See what else you can dig up and keep Newark informed, will you?"

"Certainly," he said. "Oh, and one other thing."

"What?"

"You aren't only on the 'A' list over there now. You're the top name. An assigned target."

"How about that," I said and hung up.

I went up to my room, kicked off my clothes, climbed into the shower, and after I sluiced down good, flopped on the bed in my shorts. For a little while I lay there with my hands behind my head, putting everything through my mind again.

The problem was simple enough. Get Gabin Martrel to talk. If Rondine made the contact and he knew Sonia was safe, that ought to do it. Maybe. If it worked out we'd have the answer soon. But there was something screwy involved. I couldn't put my finger on it at all. Something kept sticking out of my mind like a splinter I could feel but couldn't locate.

I dozed off like that, a frown on my face, my brain going through the computations trying to throw out the answer. When the phone rang I looked at my watch, saw I had been asleep about ten minutes and picked up the receiver. This I didn't like at all. My regular contacts had already been made and nobody else knew where I was.

The desk clerk answered and said, "Sir, there's a young lady on the way up to your room. Are you sure you want to see her?"

"What does she look like?"

"Quite pretty."

"No sweat," I told him and hung up grinning. My doll Rondine had made the contact with Martrel and was bringing home the bacon.

So she'd win a prize.

Before I could get into my clothes, there was a light tap on the door and I crossed the room, turned back the lock and opened it.

And damn near died for my mistake.

If I didn't have the habit of staying to one side with the lights off the first two shots from the silenced gun would have caught me right in the middle of the gut. He was a big guy with a half grin of pleasure on his swarthy face that was a momentary thing that went with overconfidence, and before he caught the miss and could back away to get another one in, my hand slapped the gun aside and I had his wrist with the other one.

I got him in the room with a sudden jerk that pulled him off balance in close where I wanted him and in spinning him around his feet hit the door and slammed it shut.

My fingers got his neck, dug in as I spun sideways and caught the knee that was intended for my groin on my thigh, then dipped behind him, pulled and flipped him over my back to smash on the floor. As soon as I pulled my hands away he tried to scramble up but I got him in the face with two hard chops that broke bone and left the slimy feel of blood on my knuckles.

He tried to scream then, knowing what was coming, but I didn't give him the chance. He had his and lost it. Now it was mine. I could feel his hands pounding at my head but didn't give a damn. All I did was slam into him with everything I had until he was making little bubbling noises and suddenly he went limp with his hands at his sides, moaning softly.

I shifted positions, got my knee on his throat and held it there. All it would take was a sudden pressure and he had a broken neck. "How did you find me?"

In the reflected glow from the lights of the city outside I

began to see his face. What was left of it. His eyes came open and there was pure terror there. I put a little more weight on his throat and his eyes went wider, bulging out at me. Then I took the pressure off enough so he could speak. "Knew . . . you'd think . . . of the clothes. Waited . . . followed you."

I nodded. I was getting clumsy. I should have figured the clothes stuffed in the window well would be a plant as much as they were a hiding place.

Then I saw his eyes and the terror was gone. It was all hatred, even through the blood. It wasn't sudden death after all, and I'd be the red-blooded American type with sportsmanship showing all the way through and would try for capture, interrogation and whatnot with the indignity of the just.

And he made his next mistake when he found the knife somewhere and tried to drive it into my back but missed and laid my leg open and committed suicide the hard way because in reflex I buckled and all my weight went down on my knee and with a dull crunching sound his neck broke so he died wondering what had happened.

I rolled off him, grabbed at the cut and got into the bathroom. I washed it out, tore up a towel and laid it over the wound and taped it down tight. Then I got dressed in a hurry, flipped the light on and looked at the guy.

He was a pro, all right. There wasn't a thing on him at all. The gun was a .32 with a hand-tooled silencer and I let it lay right beside him where it had fallen.

I picked up the phone, got the desk clerk and said, "You see a nice-looking broad coming up this way?"

In a bored tone he answered, "No woman has come in during the last thirty minutes."

"You didn't call me?"

"No, sir. I simply put through an outside call to your room."

"Okay, thanks."

Cute trick. They knew about Rondine and after following me here, used her as a blind calling from the phone booth downstairs. My error. I should have remembered what the desk clerk's voice sounded like. I'd have to remember that the next time.

As fast as I could I got my stuff together. If the dead guy had notified anybody else they could be waiting for him to check back. Or they could send somebody else.

Downstairs I pulled the same stunt I did the last time, getting a bellhop to pay off my bill, then went out the back way. I cut around the street, checking the cars around the hotel, but didn't find anybody parked for a quick getaway. That didn't mean a thing though. They could be holed up in a saloon, spotted in any of the buildings or ducked back in a doorway.

When I made sure I wasn't traveling with a tail on me I grabbed a cab and had him swing over to Wally Gibbons' apartment. He wasn't going to like it a bit, but I didn't have a choice.

And I was right. He glowered at me from a half-opened door, started to say something, then motioned for me to come in. He stood there in his pajamas, hands on his hips and watched me toss the suitcase in a corner and said, "You know what the penalty is for harboring a fugitive?"

"So I'll even the score. There's a dead man in my old room at the Brigham Hotel."

His mouth dropped open and he leaned back against a chair. "Man, you're nuts! You kill him?"

"Sure I did."

"Then why tell me? You know where that puts me? I have knowledge of a crime and . . ."

"Knock it off, will you? So call the cops and say you got an anonymous tip on the killing. I want them on it right away anyhow."

"In the pig's neck I will. They know I've had contact with you and keep giving me the fisheye. They'll identify you over there and put two and two together. Then I'm slammed in the cooler fast. Look, Tiger . . ."

"You look," I said coldly. "This is a matter of national security. Let Dave Severn blow the whistle then. Minutes are going to count. The guy shot at me and the police will find the bullets. The answer is pretty plain right there. I want this thing screaming in the papers. The more light we can put on it the more we're going to bottle up the other side." I gave him the details and added, "Their agents are going to know about me and Rondine from the last operation. They used her as a decoy in this. What's bad is that they may be tailing her and can use her as a lever with me."

He watched me a bit, then said, "Suppose they did, Tiger. Suppose you had a choice between the national security and Rondine. What then?"

"I'd let her die, buddy," I said calmly.

He nodded then and got up and picked up the phone. He called Dave Severn and told him to look into it. When he finished I buzzed Charlie Corbinet and laid it on the line for him too. He cut me off, told me to call back in five minutes so he could alert a team from the agency and when I reached him again he said, "It's gone too far, Tiger."

"Not yet it hasn't."

"There's a total effort out on you now. Hal Randolph and the others want to talk to you."

"Oh, great."

"They'll find you one way or another. Albert Cutter reported that he suspected Rondine of getting away from him for a time."

"Tough."

"There was more, my friend."

"Oh?"

"He wasn't the only one watching her apartment. Although he couldn't be sure he thought another party was on a stakeout too. He couldn't leave his post to check it out, but Cutter's a guy with a sharp eye and a lot of feeling for the game. He's reported Rondine as going back to her apartment, but a call there didn't rouse anybody, so he thinks she's left there again, probably out another exit than the one he was watching."

"Thanks, Colonel," I said and put the phone back.

Possible error again. CIA had one man staked out on orders to watch her or nail me. Not two or more. Just one man. But the other side wouldn't be short of manpower and it wouldn't have been a simple routine assignment. If she left by an exit they had covered they could have gotten to her anyplace.

"Wally . . ."

"No," he said bluntly. "Whatever it is . . . no."

I didn't accept it. "They have Martrel in City General Hospital. Rondine was going to make a contact there. It's no secret he's in a room under guard and you have a good excuse for checking it out. Look around to see if you can spot her."

"No."

"Get her to call me at once . . . and for Pete's sake, stay with her. Don't let her out of your sight. If you have to, get her under a police guard. I'll stay here and wait for you to call."

"No," he said again, but he was already getting dressed. When he got to the door he looked back at me disgustedly and said, "Oh, hell."

As soon as he left I called our city relay to have Newark Control call me so there wouldn't be any long-distance calls showing on Wally's bill and exposing the number over there. Five minutes later Virgil Adams called back, waited for the ID, and when I gave it and my report, said, "The head office called, Martin Grady personally again. The L.A. group pulled something out of the hat. When they were in Mexico they crossed tracks with Spaad Helo. He worked with a film outfit down there that was doing a documentary on the political situation. He speaks the language perfectly and got in with faked papers as an electrician to gain entry into certain buildings where they think he photoed some files. It was after he took off suddenly that the agents took a chance and checked him out."

"So what's the lead?"

"He had a curious call from the States that was monitored by a switchboard operator on the government payroll. She was also on ours. It came from an office in the Tomlinson Building on Broadway, a pay station in the lobby."

"What was the message?"

"It was in a foreign language, but the few American words she got were *immediately, Martrel,* and *killed.*"

"How'd they know it was Spaad?"

"Because he left a memento behind, a ring he cracked the onyx in and was having repaired. The jeweler tried to do him a favor and get on a movie set at the same time by delivering it personally against orders. The inscription read *Spaad from Anna.* Our man saw it, made the jeweler take it back and the place is staked out in case he ever tries to pick it up."

"Thanks. I'll case the Tomlinson Building."

"You might not find anything. It's a series of six public phones, that's all. Martin Grady thinks it's important because the day the call was made it was storming here. The caller might have had orders to call from outside but decided against it and made the call from his own building."

"A regular comedy of errors and that's the way you win a ball game," I told him as I hung up.

I pulled a chair up to the window, propped my feet on the sill and lay there looking out into the night. I let my eyes close and fell asleep like that, thinking.

From a long distance off I heard the insistent shrill of a bell and jerked awake. For a second the sunrise streaking in the window was almost blinding, and I looked at my watch. A little past six.

I picked up the phone. Wally said, "Tiger?"

"Here."

"The water's getting hotter."

"You clear?"

"I'm in a pay station in the hospital lobby."

"Where's Rondine?"

"Being interrogated by some Feds. She was dressed as a nurse and got past the cop into Gabin Martrel's room, carrying a tray. She would have made it if she didn't get stuck in the crapper where she was changing clothes, by a few nurses who came in to gab."

"How'd they locate her?"

"Because someone sent a beautiful potted plant up to Martrel's room. He's been getting flowers steadily and it would have been missed if one of the sharper Feds hadn't gotten curious. Seems like he'd come across a similar situation once before. Under the dirt was a timed gimmick that would have filled the room with cyanide gas and knocked him off in a hurry. They threw a block on the entire hospital and although they didn't get the delivery boy, they nailed Rondine in the crapper. The cop on the door identified her and so did a couple of the male patients."

"She talking?"

"Like a clam, but she's in for a rough time. They're pulling out all the stops. Look, clear out of my place, will you?"

I didn't answer him. I put the phone back gently and went back to watch the sun come up over the apartments.

Now they could get to me. She'd be *persona non grata* and back to England away from me if they didn't charge her with something else. But at least she had made the contact with Gabin Martrel.

I left my suitcase there, went downstairs and started the long walk over to Charlie Corbinet's place. When he opened the door I could tell from his eyes that he knew the score.

"Come on in, Tiger," he said. "I was waiting for you."

I stepped in and closed the door. "Tell Randolph I'll talk to them. One condition."

"He won't accept any conditions."

"Then tell him to go to hell."

Charlie shrugged and walked into the room. "I'll offer your condition anyway."

"Get the heat off Rondine. She has no part of this."

"Maybe not, but the agency wants further in and will go to any means to get it. You should know that."

"Nuts."

"I know Randolph."

"Okay, Colonel, then we'll talk my way."

"No phone. He wants to see you personally."

"Natch. I'll have a car pick you and Randolph up here at four this afternoon. Where you go and what the action will be is my business. He'll get to see me."

Charlie grinned and I knew what he was thinking. "He might want someone else in tow."

"He can bring an army for all I care. If he's expecting to throw an arrest on me he's got another think coming."

"Just like the old days, eh?"

"Damn right."

"We'll be ready at four." He held the door open for me and winked. Behind him on the wall were all those mementos of a time long dead, war souvenirs . . . guns, knives and gadgets we had used in the same effort before the world went screwier than ever. Some of them he had used personally. Some I had used. Most of the guys the guns belonged to died back there, and only a few of us were left now.

It didn't take long to make the arrangements I needed. Martin Grady had the funds, equipment and contacts to do almost anything. The car would be ready and in case one of them brought along an electronic beeper that another car could receive and tail, a scrambler was installed that would wash it out. Two other cars would be ready to stall traffic if they tried a normal tail by automobile and a triple check was ready if necessary. I had to grin at the preparations. Martin Grady didn't want to lose me to any jail cell just yet.

Meanwhile I had most of a day to operate in.

The Tomlinson Building was one of the older edifices packaged in a row between theaters in the middle Forties. In the lobby it was like a lot of the others, a newsstand inside the entrance, an office directory on the wall, a bank of public telephones and three elevators. Propped against the wall was a tired-looking old guy about sixty in a worn starter's uniform, and from the clientele using the building it didn't seem any prosperous businesses were going on there.

I looked over the directory, not expecting to find anything, then went to the phone booths, got out the Manhattan book, and began to look up each name on the wall systematically. It took over an hour, what with a lot of breaks to let somebody else at the phone book and occasional curious stares from the starter, but when I was finished I had three offices that weren't listed in the phone book and that, for a business, is strictly offbeat.

During a lull in the lobby traffic I went up to the starter with a folded twenty-dollar bill in my hand. He saw the long green and the number on the bill; his hostile expression turned friendly instantly as he plucked the money out of my fingers like a magician.

"It's too much for whatever you want around here, mister, but you're buying."

I let him see the three office numbers I had written down. Prado Products, F. I. Besser, and Fountain's Mail Orders.

He nodded sagely, squinted at me and said, "I know you ain't a cop."

"Let's say I'm doing research."

"Going to be trouble?"

"Not if I can help it."

"So Besser's a bookie. Everybody around here knows that."

"Why no phone? How can he operate?"

"You kiddin', mister? He's got a dozen up there but ain't none in the phone book."

I scratched off F. I. Besser. "What about the other two?"

He made a wry face, turned and pushed a buzzer on the wall to start one of the elevators going up. "Don't know about them. See people coming in and out sometimes. Fountain's gets plenty of mail and sends plenty out and I think he's legit. Little guy trying to get along, most likely. Small operator."

"No phone there either?"

"His operation doesn't need a phone. All he needs is some-body to tote a mail sack."

"That leaves Prado Products."

"Got me there, friend. Don't know nothin' about that bunch."

"Bunch?"

"Sure. About half-dozen in there, in an' out a few times a week. They run dolls up there sometimes and get booze sent up. I see film cans goin' in and out sometimes too, and like I'm not sayin' for sure, I bet they can make some pretty pictures there if you want to." He leered at me and added, "Couple of the dames went there are hookers from uptown."

"Nice."

"Happens all over," he shrugged.

"They there now?"

"Hell, none of them places open today. So far I ain't seen

none of 'em, and when they ain't in by now they ain't coming."

I grinned at him. "Think I can take a look around there?"

"That'll cost you fifty," he said.

When I gave him two twenties and a ten, he went to an anteroom down the hall, came back and pressed two keys in my hand. "They'll do it unless they added other locks to the offices. Just remember, I never saw you before in my life."

"You keep it in mind, too," I told him.

"Sure, seventy bucks' worth." He pointed toward an elevator. "That one's going up next."

My extra fifty didn't buy me anything more than goodwill. Although the keys worked in the locks, both places had other locks added. They were standard tumbler types that took a little while to open with Ernie's magic picks because I had to stop every time the elevator came up or I heard a door open.

I took Prado Products first, got in and closed the door. The inside had a barrel bolt and a chain attachment in addition to the others, and it was easy to see why. From the equipment and props lying around, Prado Products was in a touchy business, and the starter downstairs had put his finger right on it. Besides the usual equipment for shooting 16-mm. film, they had a processing set up and over in the corner was a covered tub with an acrid odor of acid. I knew what that was for. If a raid was pulled, any film could be dropped in and destroyed before an entry could be made.

They hadn't left anything around I could put my finger on. There wasn't a shred of paper work or a file anywhere. One rack contained rolls of unexposed film and a closet held the cameras along with odds and ends of clothes for participants in the filming.

When I finished the rounds of the rooms I went out, locked the door behind me and went up two flights to the office whose glass door had *Fountain's Mail Orders* across it in gold leaf. It took even longer to get that door opened because the traffic on the floor was heavier, but after thirty minutes the last lock clicked open and I walked in.

There was paper work here, all right. On two tables were stacks of mail with half-sorted piles for easy opening. A spot check of the postmarks showed most of them from the Midwest and South, all rural areas, with very few from the large cities.

It was easy to see the operation. Fountain simply advertised in some of the more lurid-type magazines and papers, offering either household gimmicks or women's bikini bathing suits and bizarre underwear and stockings. He bought wholesale from a New York firm and shipped it out at a hundred percent markup. It looked like he had a good thing going for him.

In the desk was a book of stamps, a pad listing all the repeat customers with sizes and addresses, sheafs of orders stapled together and a dozen letters desiring special requests. I went through everything he had and came up with nothing.

Whoever had used that phone downstairs had come in from someplace else, and Martin Grady's guess had been a bum one. I went out, locking up behind me, screened myself in a bunch on the elevator and didn't bother saying so long to the starter. It might have cost me some more loot.

At ten after five I picked up the car Newark Control had ready for me, turned north up the West Side Highway and crossed the George Washington Bridge into Jersey. I turned right on the Palisades Parkway, cut off at the interconnection fifteen minutes up and found the address that had been prepared. I parked the car, made sure the exit was clear and sat back to wait.

It was almost dark when I heard the other car pull up and a key go in the lock of the door on the other side of the room I was in. There were four voices in all. One I recognized as Charlie Corbinet's and another was Hal Randolph, making biting comments about the arrangement. When they sat down at the table, I flipped the toggle switch on the box beside me, saw the red light glow on and said through the intercom, "Throw your guns over against the wall, gentlemen."

Charlie laughed, but two pieces skittered across the floor. The light still stayed on.

"One more. Let's go."

There was a whispered discussion, then another followed the rest and the light blinked off. I opened the sliding panel in the wall and sat looking at them through the steel bars that separated us. They turned with that intense look of frustration, glowering at me, and Charlie said, "There's a metal detector under the table, Hal."

Randolph didn't answer him. His eyes bored into mine and he said, "Damn it, Mann, this is enough. You've had it!"

"Not yet, buddy. Now let's talk."

"You know what charges you're facing?"

"Plenty. If I don't deliver that is."

"Under any conditions. This is interference with ..."

"You couldn't make Martrel talk, could you?"

Randolph and the other two looked at each other. I had never seen either one of them before, but like the rest, they came out of a mold together. Both of them were in their middle thirties, with sharp eyes and a cut to their demeanor that put them above average.

"Who are your friends?"

Before Randolph could answer, Charlie said, "For the time being, call them Smith and Jones. They're from Washington."

The one called Smith said, "He doesn't need any details."

The Colonel's voice was cutting now. "Don't play him down. He's got the picture already."

Hal Randolph shifted in his chair. "We're holding your fiancée, Mann. She's crossed the line too."

"Just try to keep her," I said. "When . . ."

"There will be no trading," he said bluntly. "One way or another, we'll get to you."

"And the true picture can go to hell, right?"

"And what is the true picture, Tiger?" Jones said quietly.

"To get Gabin Martrel to talk."

"Really?"

The way he said it made me sweat cold. It was too easy and he meant what he said.

He knew he had gotten to me and added, "Suppose I tell you we know what Martrel knows and merely would like confirmation."

"Balls."

Jones waved a hand casually. "Then let me tell you something. We are releasing Gabin Martrel in a few days."

I stared at him. "After two attempts were made on his life?"

"Why not? Once he's released, it will be assumed that he had told us everything."

"You still don't have anything on the *Beltov Project* or OONA-3," I said.

"What makes you think so? With your experience I would think you'd realize our organization is fairly efficient. We have people inside their governments the same way they have theirs here."

"You're turning that guy out to die, buddy."

"We don't think so."

"The hell you don't." I grinned at him then. "What did you want with me?"

Hal Randolph leaned forward, his mouth tight across his teeth. "Four dead people and you're involved."

"You know the score, mister. The Colonel gave you the poop."

"The point is, Mann, that you've gotten involved with a Commie cell and stirred up things past the point of no return. You have something going for you we want to have."

I nodded, still grinning. "Tell me again about the efficiency of your agency."

"You'll see it now when your fiancée gets thrown in jail."

I could play the game of innuendoes too. I said, "You want Spaad Helo, don't you?"

Again there was that quick exchange of glances. Only Charlie Corbinet smiled a little. "What do you know, Mann?" Randolph asked.

"He's in this country," I said.

"We know that. He's pulled in key people with him. Killers. We want to break up that cell and get the personnel."

"And you think I have something that might lead you there. You want to pick my brains and run it through the computers until you get an answer."

Randolph and the others sat there silently.

"If there was time I'd let you do it. It might cost me, but I wouldn't hesitate. With all your manpower and equipment you might come up with something, but like I said, there just isn't enough time."

Randolph finally let his lips relax into a belligerent smile. "There will be for your broad, Mann. Plenty of time. Like ten years maybe, all behind bars."

He had me and I knew it and I couldn't fumble for an answer. While I reached back into my mind for a curve to throw I looked at each one in turn, playing the game all the way. All I had was a name Virgil Adams had given me the first day and I let it go.

I said, "You let Rondine go and maybe I'll be nice and drop *Project Valchek* in your lap."

I'd hit it all right. I didn't expect the sudden tight-lipped fury that swept like a mask across Randolph's face or the instant reaction of the other two whose eyes became as hard as crystal while every muscle in their bodies tightened. Only the Colonel seemed to retain his original expression, but I could read the signs in his face. *Maybe you went too far this time, Tiger boy. Now you may be in for it. You threw them a bomb.*

But I said it and I pushed it all the way. "You get the heat off Rondine. I want her out tonight. Then maybe we'll have another talk." I slammed the cover over the grill, backed away while they made a scramble for their guns and went through the door to the alley and out to my car. It was going to take them fifteen minutes before the hidden time lock on their door opened unless they wanted to break their shoulders trying to batter it down.

But the Colonel would tell them. We had pulled this before together years ago.

Rain had moved in under cover of darkness and slicked **8**
the city. Cabs made an unending stream of color in the
streets, and those walking stayed close to the buildings
or headed toward the subway entrances at a fast clip. I left the
car in a garage where it would be picked up and got over to
Wally Gibbons' apartment.

He almost slammed the door in my face, but I pushed my
way in and locked it behind me.

"Tiger . . ."

"I know, buddy. I got the word. I'll grab my clothes and
clear out. All I want to know is where they're holding Rondine."

"IATS has her in detention in the Carboy Building. They'll
have you, too, if you go near there. Every cop in the city is
looking for you, and buddy, I'm not looking for any accessory
charges, so blow, my good, troublemaking friend, get out of
my life until the air clears."

"Okay, relax. Did Dave Severn get his story?"

"Sure he did, and a lot of trouble too because he wouldn't
reveal his source of information. He was lucky he could come
up with a fast story. Me, I'll stick to my Broadway column
where all the characters stay alive for a while. With you
everybody gets killed."

"Cut it," I said. "Did you call the Treasury Department?"

"They said they'd look into it and report back. They didn't
like the idea of anyone nosing into their business."

"Baloney. They haven't any choice here."

I pulled my raincoat out of the bag, found the extra clips

for the .45 and dropped them in my pocket. "I'll leave the suitcase here."

"Fine," he said sourly as I got out of there.

Downstairs I called Newark Control and asked Adams about the *Valchek Project*. So far he hadn't heard anything except a late call from London that put it in an important status. I told him I'd call back later and hung up.

I got down to the Carboy Building before Randolph and his two friends arrived. Someplace along the line they had dropped Charlie off. The cabbie picked to stand by had a new bill in his pocket and the off-duty sign down in case somebody tried to flag him and knew what he was supposed to do. When Rondine came out of the building I was going to stay below the window level while he pulled up and waved her in.

If the Soviets had had one tail on Rondine, they'd have another. They knew what they were after and how to get it and she was as much a key factor now as I was. I doubted if they'd try for a hit, but if they got their hands on her it could be a lot worse. Now that they had lost me there was one way they could get back to me again.

They took a good hour before they released her. Twenty minutes before that I saw Albert Cutter and another man come out and deploy to their stations while a two-year-old sedan slid into place across the street ready to tail her. Until Cutter gave a minute wave with his finger I couldn't be sure who they were, then I grinned, got out of the shadows and went back to the cab. The driver was all primed and grinning from ear to ear. He was a great one for excitement, but I had a hard time keeping him quiet.

Right on the hour I saw her come out, signaled the driver and ducked down. He was there before she reached the curb, the door open like any cabbie picking up a fare in the rain, and just as she saw me I yanked her in, pulled the door shut and the cab took off with squealing tires.

Everything seemed to happen at once. Another cab had the same idea and had cut diagonally across the street from where it was parked and tried to slice into our rear end. I had one quick glance at a hard, ferret-faced driver and a bland, yet somehow cruel guy in the back before my driver had wrenched his way out of there. The sedan across the street saw the action, tried an intercept of us both and missed but succeeded in delaying the other cab a half block. It got loose while the sedan was slued sideways and came up hard be-

hind us, breaking right through the red light of the inter-
section.

At first I thought it was accidental until the streetlights
showed me Colonel Corbinet's face in a momentary glow of
pleasure, then the car he was driving came out of the second
street down, going with the green, caught the cab in a trap
and drove it to the curb. Before it had stopped both driver
and passenger were out and running, with horns going crazy
all over the place.

I put the .45 I had in my hand back in the holster and
hoisted Rondine and myself to the seat. Up front the driver
had lost his hat and was sweating down the back of his neck.
For the first time he couldn't say anything. He kept looking in
the rearview mirror at me, wondering if the press card I had
flashed on him was the real thing or not.

When she could speak, Rondine said, "What was that all
about?"

"You picked up a double tail, sugar. One would have been
rough enough."

Damn, she could stay cool. All the British reserve was there
still, and right in the middle of trouble she could stay imper-
turbable.

I said, "Sorry you got picked up. It couldn't be helped."

She smiled and touched my hand. "It wasn't as bad as what
almost happened to you."

"Who spilled it?"

"*They* told me back there."

"Oh?"

"I was too scared for you to be scared for myself any
longer."

I nodded and ran my finger along her neck. "When you
saw Martrel . . ."

"He . . . well, he started to shake. He changed. He grabbed
the picture, kissed it and put it under the covers. I told him
she was all right and he seemed to accept it, then he became
frightened. He insisted he wanted to speak to her or see her."

"Is there a phone in his room?"

"Yes, I saw one."

"Maybe we can arrange it. How do you get to the place
where you left the girl?"

She gave me directions quickly and concisely, and I took it
all down mentally. I knew the general area well enough and
getting there wouldn't be a problem. I told the cabbie to drop
us off a few blocks away from Wally Gibbons' place, slipped

him an extra ten for good luck, took Rondine by the arm and steered her down the street and into his building.

My buddy almost choked when he saw her at the door and turned white when I came in behind her. The action was getting too much for him, and he showed it. Almost tiredly he said, "Come on, Tiger, lay off me."

"I remember when you were a reporter, Wally."

"Sure, I was younger then and my heart could take it. I'm too old to take a rap now. Maybe it's a game with you and you get paid for it, but I got a little old job I enjoy and until you came back swinging I was enjoying life. Now I'm afraid to open the door. What is it this time?"

"Keep her here for now."

"Like hell," he said and sprawled in a chair.

"She's a target, Wally."

He opened his eyes, looked at me, then her. He knew what I meant. "For sure?"

"For sure."

"And you?"

"I can take care of myself."

"Who's going to take care of me?"

"You can always go on Martin Grady's payroll," I told him.

"Not when I'm dead." Then he shrugged and held out his hands. "Okay, I'll play sucker once more. But just once more, remember. After tonight it's quits. Find somebody else."

"Thanks, Wally." But he wasn't as unhappy as he seemed. At least he'd have something to look at while I was gone. I picked up the phone, called the rental agency and had them send a car over. While we waited I briefed Wally on the late details and told him about them getting ready to release Martrel.

"You think it's a blind?"

"Probably. They'll keep him covered as much as they can, but I don't think they'll be able to do it. Killers always have the edge, and they don't care who gets in the way. They'll have that hospital covered and with him being a public figure and in the news there isn't a chance he can move unobserved."

"Our people can stay with him."

"How about Dallas?"

He thought about that a minute and bobbed his head. "What are you planning?"

"If they're going to release him, maybe I can get his girl to talk him into staying under guard. He's important enough to demand it if he wants to."

The rental agency had said ten minutes and the time was up. I said I'd see them, went downstairs and waited in the lobby until a guy in white coveralls came in with the agency's name stenciled on his back. I took the papers, signed them and handed over the deposit with an extra five for him to take a cab back to the garage.

All the way up the parkway to the Connecticut Turnpike, I kept running things through my mind, looking for loose ends. There was one, all right, or I wouldn't have that funny feeling that something was wrong. You start with an impending marriage and end up with murder instead. The whole damn business was too scrambled, including the first day. *Clement Fletcher,* I kept thinking, *that's another death to add to the list. Whatever I touched. Or whoever came near me.*

I turned off the turnpike, picked my way through a residential section and headed toward the Sound. The rain had picked up and drummed against the car, sweeping in waves in front of my headlights. Rondine had laid the course out well and it was easy to follow directions. I came to the big tree enclosed by the iron fence she had described, took the left fork, following it east to its end, then when the bank of trees started, found the driveway between the stone pillars and picked my way up the gravel drive.

I saw the one light on in the house through the bushes and tall oaks, stopped the car in front of the door, turned my collar up against the rain and hopped out. When I rang there was no immediate answer, so I called out, "Tiger Mann, Sonia, open up."

The door came open on a chain lock then, and when she saw that it was me, pulled off the catch and held it open. "It is so long since I have been here. I am glad to see you."

I pushed the door shut, locked it and whipped the rain off my hat. "Anybody been here?"

"Only those who turn on the lights and the phone." She pointed toward an archway. "Come inside, please. It is warmer there. You will dry off. Let me take your things."

I gave her my coat and hat and went over to a sideboard and mixed myself a drink. She let me finish half of it then asked, "You have heard . . . from Gabin?"

"Still in the hospital, but they're going to take him out."
She frowned. "But . . . "

"He can't afford to be on the streets. I'm going to get a call through to him, and I want you to tell him you're in safe hands and for him to stay under guard until he's talked to our people."

"Perhaps if I went there . . ."

"They tried for you once. You want them to get you two at a time? If they hit you, Martrel will never open up. Nix, kid . . . we'll do it from here. I'll drive you into town and we'll hit a pay station. They may let the call go through, but it will be monitored. If you reach him, tell him you're safe and for him to stay put. Be brief so they can't put through a tracer. They'll know the call came from this area but there are too many roads to block off so I'm not worried there."

"But if . . . they will not let me speak to him . . ."

"You say who you are. They'll put you on."

"Whatever you wish."

"Get your coat."

We went two towns over and found a pay station outside a closed gas station and I called information, got the number of the hospital from the operator, thanked her and hung up. I gave Sonia a handful of change and the number, let her get into the phone booth and stood outside with one eye on the road while she made the call.

Through the glass door I could see her, and she turned and made a hopeless gesture my way, tried to insist on something, then put the phone up. When she came out she was biting her lip. "It was a man they gave me. He tried to . . . to put me off. He said Gabin was sleeping and couldn't be disturbed and I should call back later."

"They wanted time to trace the call. Damn."

"Perhaps later we can . . ."

"No. They'll have everything bugged." I shoved her into the car out of the driving downpour. "We'll make the call in the morning from another station. We'll keep moving around and eventually they'll put you on. They'll have to."

"But he *is* safe?"

"For now."

I left the car in the same place and followed her inside. The rain had gone right through my coat, and I was soaked. So was she. The gas flames jumping in the fireplace against the artificial logs felt good against my face and I pulled off my clothes and shed my shirt and tie. Sonia looked at me approvingly and said, "If I may?"

I nodded as I stood there with my hands toward the fire.

Behind me I heard her move off out of the room.

When she came back she had on a sheer white, semitransparent negligee that blossomed around her curves and as she stood there with her hands on her hips enjoying the approving look I gave her she said, "You recognize it?"

"Rondine's?"

"Yes. I hope . . . I look as pretty . . . as she does."

"You do." I wasn't lying. Her beauty was different, a little more primitive, but there was a fiery challenge in every motion she made. Although time had taken the muscular huskiness from her there was something ripply about the way she walked, and I could see the smooth play of life along the outline of her thighs.

Beneath the white was the dark outline of the briefest underclothes with a strange raised pattern that had an exciting, exotic effect, a skimpy bra that barely covered the crest of her breasts and left a wide, wide expanse of pink skin that made me tingle to look at her. I tried to turn away, but kept looking at her out of the corner of my eyes while she curled up on the couch.

The luscious deep red of her mouth smiled at me, and there was a flush on her cheeks. Her fingers picked up the folds of the negligee, and she spread it out around her in a wide arc. "Long ago, there were not things like this. In Russia it was not . . . considered proper."

"Too capitalistic?"

"It was not considered right to display such . . . such feeling. In secret I would wear things. Never to someone else's eyes."

"On you it looks good."

She gave a funny squeal of pleasure and squirmed happily so that one lovely leg showed through the opening in the gown. "You will come sit with me?"

"Should I? I was supposed to be protecting you, gal."

"Please." There were tiny crinkles at the corners of her eyes.

"You belonged to Martrel."

"No, never, not really. I told you, we were friends."

"That's all?"

She looked down at her hands folded in her lap. "My father was killed at Stalingrad. I think it was with Gabin . . . that he was like my father."

"It's going to be tough to explain," I said.

She glanced up and nodded. "Yes. But he must know. I always knew how he felt. He must be told. It is why I came to him. He will need me for a little while then he will be all right."

I picked up my drink, finished it, put the glass down and

sat beside her. Outside the wind-driven rain beat against the windows in mourning fury and thunder rumbled like a cannon roll in the distance. A flash of lightning lit up the grounds, throwing sudden brightness into the room, and with a short cry of fright she leaned against me and buried her head in my shoulder.

"Easy. It's only a storm." I put my arm around her gently and tilted her head up. There was a little-girl quality about her eyes and the way she cringed whenever the thunder cracked overhead. Each time she moved closer and someplace in between she was warm and fresh against me and everything seemed to come apart as our mouths met. The restrained passion inside her made her lips quiver, a soft, fleshy cushion, spicy wet, that cried out for release.

Her hands took mine and pressed them against the loveliness of her body, the warmth of her radiating right through the fabric. Under my fingers her skin had the smoothness of satin, the firm resiliency of youth that moved with small nervous impulses of anticipation.

We brought the storm into the room then, one of our own making, a wild flight into a crazy world of passion that was totally unrestrained. No longer could we hear the sounds from outside and the wind and rain on the windows diminished to a soft whisper under the pounding in my ears.

There was no concept of time or distance, no remembrance of anything for an unbelievably long period, until at last we lay there together in pleasant exhaustion and let the world come back to normal. Outside there was a bluish-white flash, a crack and a hissing sound and the momentary lull that comes after a close lightning stroke before the sharp smack of thunder, and the two lamps across the room blazed bright a second then went out.

Sonia jerked under my hands as I quieted her, grabbing for my arms. I got up, disengaging her fingers. "It hit outside. Stay put. I better check it."

"Do you have to?" She sounded scared.

"Could be a fire hazard, honey. Let's not take chances."

I got my clothes on, slipped into the raincoat and ducked out the front door. I ran around to the side where the flash had come from, looking for signs of smoke or flame, found nothing until I saw the bare white of a tall pine near the house where the bark had been peeled back and seared from the intense heat. I let out a quiet curse at the strokes that broke from the overcast above every few seconds.

But I shouldn't have. One saved my skin because I had a brief glimpse of movement from a bush and time to throw myself to the ground as the snap of a gun merged with the thunder and slug buried itself in the house behind me. I shed the light tan coat as I rolled, scrambled to my feet in the direction to the right of the bushes, figuring the other one would change position too until he made sure of the hit, and then I waited until the next flash came.

I saw him before he saw me and made the leap that put him under my hands and set the gun flying into the darkness. The yell he started got strangled in his throat as I lifted him off the ground and bent him over my back. This was one guy I wanted to make talk no matter how I did it. I slammed him against the ground and grinned at the fear showing through his eyes. I picked him up, started to arch him into a position that could break his back if I wanted to, and just as I got him set the lightning came again and I saw the other one starkly clear in the nearly blinding light standing thirty feet away with a rod in his hand and his fingers tightening on the trigger. *I had seen him before in the back seat of a cab that went for me.*

Out of animal instinct I dropped as the gun went off and felt it slam into the human shield I held in front of me. The guy let out a soft, gurgling moan and went limp before I dropped him. I didn't stay there. I dodged to one side, feeling for the bushes, waiting for another burst of light to locate my man.

But with the peculiar inconsistency of the elements, it didn't come. I felt gravel under my feet, stood there trying to get my eyes adjusted to the darkness, and then I heard the sound of a car pulling away on the road outside the grounds. There wasn't any sense going in pursuit. He had too much of a start. Now we just had to get out of there.

The dead man lay where he had fallen and I checked his clothes quickly. There wasn't enough light to look for identifying marks, but I found a handful of bills and change in his pockets, a set of keys, cigarettes and a flat wallet in his inside coat pocket. I kept that and left the rest of the stuff, went inside and found a massive lighter on the sideboard, flicked it and opened the wallet.

It was a Treasury Department folder identifying the holder as Henry Buckman and his badge was pinned to the other flap. Now the stuff had really hit the fan! With a cop dead the effort would go all out with me on the receiving end.

I closed the folder and tossed it in a chair. There were two possibles though. If the guy behind the gun was another T-man who hit his partner accidentally in a try for me it would be too bad. But if they were from two separate factions and the other wasn't a T-man, but from the Soviet group, my neck was in a sling.

Sonia said from where she still crouched on the couch, "Tiger . . . what was it?"

"Nothing."

"I heard a noise."

"Forget it. Hop into your clothes. We have to clear out fast."

She didn't argue. I saw her movement in the darkness. "Yes, Tiger." The tone of my voice had been enough.

While she felt her way out of the dark room I reached the phone, picked it up and dialed Wally Gibbons' number in the city. The second time it rang, Wally answered and his voice was all shook up. I said, "Anybody on the extension?"

"No . . . they're gone."

"What happened?"

"Damn you, I'm caught in a trap."

"Just tell me what happened."

"A couple of Treasury men come up here. They wanted to know about that tip on the *Maitland*. They wouldn't tell me anything. All they did was ask questions."

"You know them?"

"Yeah, I had run into 'em before. They caught Rondine here and gave her a working-over, and when one went through her bag he found the receipts from the light and phone company from the place in Connecticut."

"Okay, okay, so what did they do?"

"Nothing. It was all questions. They didn't give out anything."

"Is Rondine still there?"

"Yeah, and they want us to stay here. We're going to have more company in the morning."

"I'll see you tomorrow."

"Forget it."

I grunted and hung up. Sonia came out carrying a suitcase, and I told her to leave it there. I took her hand and steered her out the door. She waited until we were in the car going down a darkened back road that wound up toward the turnpike before she asked me again.

I said, "They found us, kid. They put Wally Gibbons and

me together, figured I might contact him and kept a cover there. They saw me come out and tailed me here."

"But . . . couldn't you have seen them?"

"Not in this storm. He could have done the job with his lights off. He made the mistake of waiting too long before trying for his hit. The T-man got here first, saw me outside and thought I had spotted him and was there to get him. He tried for a shot, missed it and in the scuffle caught one from the other guy."

"What will happen now?"

"It's you, me and Martrel. They keep after us. We can't leave any leads behind us now. I'm going to dump you someplace safe, baby."

"But Gabin . . . they will try to kill him?" Her voice had an edge to it.

"You can lay a bet on that."

"Tiger . . . please . . . don't let them hurt him. Please, my Tiger."

"I'll do what I can. They have a guard on him right now."

"Is it enough?"

"No. They'll be releasing him shortly. They can't keep him any longer."

She touched my arm lightly, the pressure of her fingers pleading. "You will do something then?"

"Something."

Above us the sky split with the suddenness of all storms coming to an end and the pale ruby glow of a sunrise came through to warm the night. "It's breaking," I said.

"An omen. It will be a pretty day."

"I hope you're right."

We stopped and ate along the way, letting the day come on us slowly. It was a small place with an open pay phone on the wall to one side. When we finished, I handed her some change and said, "Let's make that call to the hospital again."

I went back with her while she dialed the number and heard her ask for Gabin Martrel. She held the phone away from her ear so I could hear the rough male voice that asked her business, passed her name to someone else and a series of clicks as the call went through to his room. She did what I told her to, gave him the message quickly, cutting through the rapid Russian he queried her in. I gave her the cutoff sign and she said she'd call again with more information and hung up in the middle of his chatter.

"What did he say?"

"He was very excited. He couldn't speak English even."

"It figures."

"He will do as I ask. He was very afraid for me."

"Let's get out of here."

I paid the bill, got behind the wheel and pulled away from the drive. A quarter-mile down the road a patrol car passed going the other way, wide open with the siren screaming. "They don't lose much time," I told her.

"It makes me afraid."

I reached over and switched on the radio, picking up a local station. It was right on the half hour and the early news was on. The chief message of interest was that the body of a man had been found on the premises of the Burton Selwick estate by government agents but didn't go any further. Details would be forthcoming later. So would my prints. Those and Sonia's were all over the place.

Before I hit any roadblocks, I turned into the residential section and headed for New York the hard way, fighting early-morning traffic. Once I got to the city I took the West Side Highway downtown to a drop Martin Grady kept handy in the section built up with small industries and parked the car in front of the place.

At one time it had been a garage, then had turned into a warehouse before Grady picked it up. We used it occasionally to keep equipment there, and when it was necessary, to hole up out of sight. It had a front, rear and side exits, an escape opening to the roof, and the back room was stocked with a bed and enough provisions to provide a fairly decent temporary shelter.

I took Sonia in through the side door, locked it and showed her the layout. It wasn't the best, but it would have to do. While she was going through the place, I called Newark Control, got Anderson instead of Adams who told me to see Ernie Bentley as soon as possible. He had a telephotoed picture of Spaad Helo in from Europe and wanted me to look at it. Nothing else on *Project Valchek* except that it was getting hotter. Martin Grady was under fire from another Congressional committee and my picture and description were being flashed all over the country.

"Great. What else is new?"

"We think there was another attempt on Martrel's life."

"Think?"

"Grady put another team on watching the hospital. One was in the mail room sorting out letters, picking up return

addresses on all the Martrel stuff and spotted a card that
didn't look kosher. He thought it was one of those trick jobs
Kilm Rosser used to poison that witness in Madrid . . . the kind
with the poisoned cutting edge that gets you when you open it.
He gave it to Ernie."

"I'll check it when I see him."

"Hop to it. If they miss this time they'll close in fast. I
wouldn't put anything past them." He closed the connection
then, and I stood there thinking about it.

Sonia saw the look on my face. "It is worse now?"

"They tried for Martrel again, I think."

Her breath went in with a sharp gasp. "He can't stay there!"

"Nobody knows about this attempt except us so far. They
won't have any extra guards on him."

"Take him away, please!"

"The only way is to kidnap him."

"Any way, Tiger, but do it."

"It would be better if I could convince him to cooperate.
We might make it work." I looked at her.

"He would listen to me," she said.

We made the call from a mile away, got through the
monitored setup to Martrel, but pulled a cutie when she gave
him the pitch in rapid Russian. If they had forgotten to have a
translator handy in case of the eventuality, we'd have it made.
When she hung up I hustled her out to the car, her eyes
shining. "Whatever is necessary, he will do. Gabin was over-
joyed, but he does not realize his danger."

"Will he talk to our people?"

She nodded energetically. "With me. He says when he can
hold my hand in his he will speak to them. He wants me to be
with him."

"Okay, kid, you can be part of the show then."

I dropped her at the warehouse after giving her the knock
signal. To make sure her enthusiasm didn't get the better of
her so she'd try for another call to Martrel, I pulled a hidden
switch and disconnected the phone. It was better not to take
any chances at all. Maybe she did have a father image and
maybe she did respond to passionate impulses when it hit her,
but when I saw the light in her eyes after the phone conver-
sation, I knew she had more inside her for Gabin Martrel
than she told me. Or maybe even knew about herself.

Before I left I kissed her lightly, winked and closed the
door. I turned the car in by phone, leaving it in a parking lot

with the money at the cashier's desk and walked over to Ernie Bentley's lab.

The haggard look on his face meant he had been up all night, and he pushed a chair toward me while he rummaged through his desk. "Either they get me more help or slow you jokers down a little."

"You're not getting shot at in here either, kid."

"That still doesn't get me home to my wife."

"You told me you don't need it anymore."

"Only sometimes, but when it happens I don't want to be here twenty-four hours at a stretch."

"So move her in with you."

"She thinks I'm in a simple experimental engineering job. All I need is for her to dig this deal." He came up with a picture in his hand and passed it across his desk to me. "Spaad Helo. Came out of obscure captured German war files and enlarged from a two-by-two up to ten-by-ten. Telephotoed transmission didn't add to clarification. Stick twenty years on his age, figure the ravages of time and you'll know what he looks like today."

"You do a retouch?"

"Two of them." He handed me another pair rephotographed after the work had been done. "One thinner, one heavier. Take your pick."

"I already have." I tapped the one of the heavier-looking face because I had seen it twice before. Once in the back of the taxi and once with a gun blasting in his hand in Burton Selwick's yard.

"Definite?"

"Positive," I said. "Better notify Grady. He'll want this to go in the government files, too. He can use a little good public relations at the moment." I tossed the picture back to him. "What about that letter sent to Martrel?"

"Another positive. A real gimmick, that. I'm surprised it isn't used more often. There are four different cutting edges, so you can nick yourself opening the envelope or the letter itself. The poison used is the second distillate of the Monger formula. It causes death in about thirty seconds, too fast to do anything about it once it's in you. Very few people know about those Monger experiments, so you know the level you're working on."

"I'll take a gun."

"You always did. You're not the neat type." Ernie grinned and held out three small photos. "I made up some copies of

Spaad Helo if you want to spread them around for identification purposes."

"Thanks." I stuck them in my pocket.

"You know his history, don't you?"

I nodded.

"Well, anyway, I researched his file for you. To recapitulate, the man is a pure terror. In his own way he's like you. He'll go to any length to complete an assignment. He only gets the most important. We're pretty sure he's been on some of the major blowups of world policy in the last few years and although nobody really knows him, he has access to almost anything through the Commie spy network. If we could break up that chain it would be a big job."

"You'd wash out OONA-3?"

"Exactly. If we located their line of communication we could nail the agents Since these are all highly trained personnel well-established in the States they won't be easy to replace. It could really put a crimp in Soviet espionage."

"Martrel was head of that operation."

"Ah," Ernie said, "that's the kicker. Over there nobody gets big enough to contain it all. They make damn sure of that. I'll lay odds he doesn't know more than a few agents. They operate from small independent cells under a tight command. . . . Hell, why am I telling you what you already know?"

"Go ahead, Ernie."

"Well, Martrel could know the project values, but not all those assigned to it. If we knew that we could stop any of their operations before they got started. New imports would be easy to spot, and, if they tried buying into the pinko-liberal crowd for help they'd be dealing with amateurs and that, friend, isn't the safe or practical way of handling international sabotage. But any lead is better than none; that's why Martin Grady wants Martrel to get his tongue moving."

"Maybe I can oil it up for him."

"Don't tell me about it. I can't stand the bloody details."

"It might be easier than you think."

Ernie stood up and wiped a hand across his tired eyes. "Need anything?"

"No."

"Still carrying that ball-point?"

I tapped my shirt pocket. "I got it."

"Watch it. Those plastic threads for the cap don't hold too well and work loose sometime. Make sure it stays screwed down tight while it's on you."

My fingers went to the gimmick automatically, checked the cap, and when I was satisfied I wasn't a walking bomb, I shoved the chair back. Ernie had a typewriter in the corner and I tapped out my report for Central and handed it to him. "Get this in for me, okay?"

"Sure." He folded it and shoved it in his desk.

I picked up the phone, scowled at it and dialed Wally Gibbons' number. When he came on his voice barked a curt "Hello" and I said, "Tiger, baby. Your company arrive yet?"

He didn't sound a bit friendly anymore. "Oh yes, old buddy. They've been here all right. So has my editor and lawyers from the paper. They're very interested in my activities, specially as how they concern you."

"Anyone there now?"

"At the moment we are under what amounts to house arrest. Just a gentle reminder from the Treasury men to stay put while they do some more prowling. One of the IATS men was up here with them and down on the street a nice CIA boy sits in his car."

"Albert Cutter," I said.

"He stops up every so often to check on your visiting girl friend. I don't like it."

"Don't knock the attention, Wally. It's one way of keeping your hide on. Nobody will be making a play for you if they stay close."

"Listen, tough guy, I want no involvement at all. You know what I mean? These Treasury guys . . ."

Interrupting him, I said, "They locate anything on the *Maitland?*"

"No, big mouth, and that's exactly what's got me in this damn mess. Nothing. They don't like bum steers. They went all over the ship, held it up from sailing, with the shipowners squawking right up to Washington, and now they're holding it over my head. They never did pull a previous search either."

"They wouldn't give anything out if they did."

"You goofed, Tiger. You pulled a dilly."

"So did the other side."

He paused, lowered his tone and I knew he was smelling news again. "Okay, I'm in this deep already so get on with it."

I told him about the letter Martrel received and the way it was gimmicked. "Keep it quiet a little longer, and when it breaks you can have a scoop. I'll even give you the damn letter."

"You're withholding evidence," he reminded me.

"Not until somebody knows about it."

"Then why tell me? Why do I have to have guilty knowledge?"

"So you'll know you'll have something to offer when you have to go begging to get your job back. I've never known an editor or publisher yet who wasn't a sucker for a scoop, and when a simple Broadway columnist can come up with a big one it could put him in good standing."

"Well, like I said before, don't do me any favors." He slammed the phone back, muttering to himself. Even having Rondine around to look at wasn't going to make him any happier.

Ernie said, "Trouble really sticks around you, doesn't it?"

I didn't answer him. I stood there with my hand on the phone, trying to gather up the ends and put them in place. Finally I said, "I'm going to get Martrel out of that hospital, Ernie."

"How?"

"I don't know yet but it has to be done."

"Good luck. If you need any special props give me an hour to locate them."

"Sure, buddy. Keep a line open to London and see if anything comes in on that *Valchek* thing. It's got me interested. Just mentioning it flipped Hal Randolph and if it has any connection with this business or I can come up with a lead, I might get myself off the hook."

"Roger. Keep in touch. Where will you be?"

"Around town. I'll call in."

"I'll stay put," he said. "Incidentally, if you need an assist in the hospital, we're keeping those two guys on assignment. The tall redhead in the mail room is ours and so is the guy in the disposal truck. It's under the name of V. R. Sanitation Company, a blue ton-and-a-half, one of Grady's affiliates."

"Good deal. I'll keep it in mind."

I met Charlie Corbinet in a small restaurant on Second Avenue for lunch. I sat at a table in the back and watched him have a drink at the bar, checking me to see that I was clear before coming over to join me. The waiter came over, took our orders, then I said, "Thanks for the assist."

"Thought you'd need it. I was there primarily to cut out the tail Randolph had planned for you. I knew you'd set it up yourself but didn't want to take a chance. Who was in the taxi?"

"A pair of killers, Colonel. They had the same thing in mind. They're covering every possibility. What did Randolph have to say about it?"

Charlie shrugged, his weather-beaten face unperturbed. "He hit the roof naturally, but there wasn't anything he could do. When I saw the taxi I got the picture and tapped it out of the way. You were lucky, Tiger."

"You have to be in this business. Was the taxi stolen?"

"A couple hours earlier. The driver was eating and it was picked up from where he parked it. Trying to run down a stolen cab in New York isn't easy so they weren't worried about it. They probably were going to pull your stunt . . . getting Rondine into their cab, only you beat them out."

I reached in my pocket and pulled out one of the photos Ernie had given me. "Here's the guy in the back of the cab. It's retouched from an old ID picture the Nazis had on him, but it's the guy all right. His name is Spaad Helo."

The Colonel's eyes came up briefly from under his bushy eyebrows, studied me and went back to the photo again. "This might ease things with Randolph. You know IATS has been after him for years?"

"Uh-huh."

"He's never been identified visually before."

"Those days are gone."

"How'd you come across it?"

"Trade secrets, Colonel. Let's keep it that way for now. What happened after you clipped the taxi?"

"Both of them got away. It wasn't hard. There was a subway exit on the corner and they lit out down there. With the platforms full of people and trains on quick schedule I couldn't locate them. As it was, a cop tried to get me for leaving the scene of an accident. It took some fast work to placate him."

"Get a flyer out on Spaad Helo then. He's here in the city. He bumped that T-man out in Connecticut that has my name on it."

Charlie looked up and shook his head. "That was no T-man, Tiger."

"What?"

"I saw the report. They lifted your prints along with Sonia Dutko's, and a cross-check came right to the office. The body is still unidentified."

I scowled at the drink in my hand, beginning to get a funny

idea in my head. "Can you get me a body shot of the guy? A head close-up will be enough."

"Sure. Where do you want it sent?"

"Get it delivered over to Stanton's Bar on Broadway. Leave it with Ron."

"Think you have a make on him?"

"Maybe. I want to show it around. If anything comes up, you'll get it right away. Do me a favor and stand by. I may need a fast gun hand and if one of our own people isn't available I'll call on you."

His eyes were half closed as he listened to me and I knew he was drifting back across time and space to those years ago, putting them all together and seeing in me what I was seeing in him. At last he nodded, then reached over and tapped the back of my hand. "Think you're big enough to take advice?"

"When it's asked for," I said easily.

"You won't ask for this but you'll get it anyway."

"I'm listening."

"Drop Martin Grady. Get out of the business. It was great when the job had to be done and it was an all-out effort. It was fine when you were alone and so full of hate nothing mattered, but you're changed, Tiger. You have a woman waiting and you're not alone anymore."

"The job still has to be done."

"Let somebody else do it. There are others who *are* alone and can hate like you used to. They're young and fast and have all the capabilities that you and I ever had. Given enough training, experience and luck and they could fill our shoes with no trouble at all."

"You don't break old habits, Colonel."

"If you don't break this one it'll break you. Sooner or later you'll have Rondine on your mind when you should be thinking of something else and you'll die, or you'll consider her first before taking the gambles you used to take and somebody else will die instead. I saw it happen and so did you. Cut out before it's too late. There's always room for somebody like you in civilian life."

"Not like me, Colonel. There will never be room. I'll always be on the Red 'A' list and somebody will always be looking for me, so whether I like it or not I'm still involved. I couldn't go into one of your agencies because of guys like Randolph. They'd always remember my background and keep me cut out. No matter where I turn from now on I'll have to keep my back covered and if I want to stay alive I'll have to keep in practice. Just like you, friend, it's something I have inside me I can't burn out. In my head are names and places and faces I'll see some-day and recognize as enemies that have to be destroyed and when that happens the switch gets turned on and it will happen."

His eyes never left mine and I could almost taste the regret that he had in them. "You were going to resign before this got started."

"That's what I said."

"But you never really meant it."

"Okay, so I won't fool you or myself. I would have turned in a letter and taken off with Rondine. For a while we'd be happy then I'd get that urge or an urgent call from somebody or fall into a lead on something still open in the files and that would bust it."

"She won't accept it, you know."

"Then it's over. She takes me as I am or cuts out. This old soldier's been around a little too long. The mold took too well."

"I'm sorry for you, Tiger."

Unconsciously, I grinned at him. "I used to be sorry for myself. I like it better this way. I got it all clear now." I jabbed a forefinger his way. "You aren't the best one to give advice, you know."

"At least I'm alone. I have nobody to answer to or be responsible for. I'm with an authorized agency that gives me pleasure to work with and they can utilize my experience."

"You're quibbling, old buddy," I told him. "You're making excuses for yourself. You'd like nothing better than to be ten years younger and as tough as you used to be. You just can't mellow out of action. The next time you use a gun and get somebody on the end of it you won't be thinking of the little speech you just made."

"I hope you don't either."

"Habits are hard to break." I picked up the check, shook hands with Charlie Corbinet and walked out. I knew he was watching my back in the mirror, envying the action all the way.

On the street I turned north and started walking. I could big-mouth it back there to the Colonel, but what was the real answer? I was going to have to tell her and I knew what would happen. I knew the expression she'd have in her eyes and could almost hear her words. We had both done our bit and it was enough. We had to grab what time was left for ourselves before it was too late. She would echo Charlie's thoughts and turn them on me and there really wouldn't be any answer at all. Just a quick break and it was over.

Maybe some were lucky after all . . . and others just as unlucky. I would hate even harder then with the total hatred of disgust thrown in. I'd look for the fast way out and never be able to make it because I was just a little bit better and a small bit quicker than the other ones.

So far.

One day I'd see a blinding exit of my own and it would be done. The disgust and hate would be wiped out in an instant and there would be nothing more to think about because the dead don't think. Or it could be worse. The big hit would never come and I'd have to live without her as I had all those years since the war.

Could I afford to lose her twice?

Was it worth it?

Up ahead a pair of cops were talking on the corner, hands behind their backs, teetering on their toes. With professional casualness they screened every face that went by, registering their features, discarding them without knowingly doing so. I was going to cross the street, but there was another one there talking to a D.O.S. man on a mechanized sweeper.

The theater that was between me and the corner advertised a double bill, old movies I had seen before, but I didn't want to stretch the odds. I forked over eighty cents, picked up my ticket, found a seat in the back row and slept through all the entertainment.

At seven-thirty I uncramped myself, went outside, made a cursory check for cops and when I didn't spot any, started north again. At a diner I had a quick supper, then got in a crosstown subway, transferred and went north to the station under City General Hospital.

The evening crowd was light and I fell in with it, making the tour of the building complex. The place took up an entire city block with a series of entrances on all sides and a double drive up the front. Both sides of the blocks surrounding it were lined with parked cars, there for the visiting hours.

It took time, but it had to be done. As I walked by I looked into each car, making sure they were empty. Each inspection had to be fast and casual, each check into the stores and bars had to be as complete as possible without wasting time. But how could I be sure? *Damn!* Someplace there would be a watcher. They wouldn't drop anything at this point. It was a time to step up the pace because it couldn't last and whoever got to him first would make the score.

I swung around the block twice. As far as I could see, nothing seemed to be out of the way, but that wasn't saying much. A good-sized team could be staked out in the area in constant motion, and it would never be noticed.

People without faces, I thought. *They'd look just like anyone else. I was one of the same breed. Only they had a file on me and here they'd be using all clean personnel, ones held for deliberate assignments like this.*

On the west side of the building I spotted the blue truck with the V. R. Sanitation Company label on the side. Apparently the driver had just completed dumping a load because he was parked and standing beside the cab having a cigarette. I went by, said the code word that identified all of us to one another and he gave the countersign of recognition.

He let me get a hundred-foot lead, then, on some pretext of his own, followed me. I heard his feet get closer, and as he passed I said, "Stand by. I'll need the truck. Keep the hood up as if you have engine trouble."

I didn't need an answer. He got the message. I watched him cross to a drugstore and I turned the corner to the front of the building thinking of how I was going to work it. There would be cops inside and any loiterer would be spotted. Whatever I did had to be easy and natural. I passed the main drive, still going over it in my mind when I heard the squeal of brakes up ahead and heard a loud voice swearing at somebody who had just gone through the traffic signal.

A car came screeching up the street, swung into the drive and came to a skidding stop. The woman got out laughing, but the man was a nervous wreck. She was minutes away from having a baby and was making a ball of it, but it wasn't funny to her husband.

I grinned a little, went back to the front entrance, up the steps and into the lobby. I was far from alone. Better than a dozen prospective fathers were sitting reading or pacing anxiously, depending on how many times they had been through the routine before. By the elevators was a uniformed patrolman and another farther down the hall by a stairwell. I kept my back to them, took up a position so I could watch the procedure and stayed put.

Every so often one of the nurses or a doctor would come down, a name would be announced and one of the fathers would take the trip back upstairs. The cops never bothered looking past the white hospital uniforms. I asked the girl at the desk where the men's room was and she smiled politely, apparently used to these nervous urges, and pointed the way.

Fifteen minutes. Then Sonia would make that call.

I washed my hands a dozen times before one of the interns came in. I took him out with one hard chop in the jaw that would keep him silent a half hour, stripped off his clothes, climbed into them and left him locked in the can. He had been carrying a clipboard and if you ever want a pass into a restricted area that's all you need. It's a psychological weapon because nobody wants anything written on a clipboard, and with a stethoscope around your neck you can manage almost anything in a hospital if you work fast enough.

I took the elevator up right past the cop, got off at the fifth floor and turned right after a quick look at the sequence of numbers on the doors. It was eleven-thirty. If Sonia were able to get the call through she would be calling now.

Down at the end the cop outside the last door looked my way speculatively, so I went in the door closest to me. A little old man looked up, smiled while I read his chart and when I smiled back, closed his eyes again. I made four rooms that way, hitting only one empty and having luck with me all the way. A nurse passed once but was too absorbed in her own thought to do more than nod absently. A pair of cleaning women came by talking up a storm and a floor polisher had started in from the other end of the hall, pushing his buffer ahead of him.

When I reached the door I wanted, I beat the cop to the question and said, "Routine check for contagious diseases. Somebody's brought something in with them. More night work."

The cop nodded, never relaxing an instant, opened the door so I could go in and stayed right behind me. I checked the chart on the bed, made a few scribbled notes on the pad, then walked to the patient.

He knew me, all right. There was a tight set to his face that gave him a peculiar expression and he was debating whether to sound off to the cop or keep quiet. I grinned, nodded toward the phone and said, "They're breathing all kinds of things around here. Even comes through the phone."

"My callers are all healthy," he told me, his face relaxing.

I went through some phony mechanics of feeling his pulse,

checking his eyes and tongue, then half turned over my shoulder. "Hand me that chart, will you?"

Unconsciously, the cop reached for the end of the bed and took his eyes off me for just a second. It was enough. It only took a minute to strip him and get Martrel into his clothes and the cop in the bed where he'd be comfortable until he reached the precinct station.

While Martrel dressed, I asked him, "What did Sonia say?"

"Not much. That she was safe and in good hands."

"She is. You ready?"

The clothes didn't fit the way they should have, but unless another cop saw him he'd pass inspection. One thing about a uniform. People don't look at the face. Martrel nodded nervously and licked his lips. "If we are caught?"

"Then my tail's in the fire, not yours. After slugging that cop it couldn't get much worse. Now relax, look natural and stay with me. I don't want to hurry. If we start to run it will attract attention, you understand?"

His smile had a big meaning in it. This kind of job had been his at one time too. "Yes, I understand."

Rather than use the elevator we took the stairwell down, staying to one side so those coming up could pass. Most of them were too absorbed in their own thoughts to give us a second notice. Cops and medics go with city hospitals and our presence there wasn't unusual. When we reached the lobby, I told Martrel to wait inside the exit, gambled that I wouldn't be spotted, and went to the men's room where I had laid out the doctor.

I crossed through the crowd that was collected around the desk asking for visitors' passes, found the men's room empty this time and opened the door where the intern was still slumped on the seat. I got dressed and hung his clothes on the hook behind the door. As I left I looked at him squatting there snoring gently with his mouth half opened, grinned and said, "Physician, heal thyself." It wasn't much thanks for what he had done for me.

The crowd was bigger now and gave me plenty of cover, but could hide others too if it hid me, but it was a chance that had to be taken. I got to the exit, waved Martrel out and he followed behind me to the main door, pushed through it and joined me on the street. If a stakeout saw us without getting an immediate make they'd be more interested in remaining unobserved than taking a closer look. Cops in uniform have that effect. Just in case, I had my hand on the butt of the .45, ready to shoot our way out of there if I had to. Martrel caught my position, and although he said nothing, looked around him carefully.

The guy in the truck saw us coming and asked no questions. He hopped off the bumper of the truck, slammed the hood, wiped his hands and got behind the wheel and started the engine. I shoved Martrel around to the other side and climbed in after him.

"Roll," I said. "Anywhere."

"Right."

I tapped Martrel. "Get that cap and jacket off. If a cop spots you in here we've had it." He acknowledged and got out of the rig, packing it in back of the seat.

The driver said, "Where to?"

"We'll have to hole up someplace and get him some clothes."

"I got a small apartment not far from here. No clothes in it though. Just some extra coveralls."

"We'll figure that angle out later. Let's use the apartment for tonight. The cops'll have a dragnet out all over the city for us and they'll be checking every means of escape. As far as you're concerned, you had some engine trouble and took the truck out to check it."

The apartment was a two-room affair in an old building near Riverside Drive. We got inside without being seen, and I told the driver to get the cop's uniform back to the hospital. He could say he picked it out of one of the trash cans, found it in the street or whatever seemed reasonable. If they checked out his story about leaving and found someone who saw the truck downstairs, it was because he needed a change of coveralls from working on the engine. He changed into fresh white ones to back up the story and took the others back wrapped around the blue police pants Martrel had had on.

Unfortunately, there was no TV or radio in the apartment so I couldn't tie into a news broadcast to keep up on developments, not that it was really necessary. Right now every agency available would be working on the thing and that hospital would be sealed off like a tomb. With IATS knowing my interest in the thing, it wouldn't take long for the cop I had slugged to make an identification. But first they'd go through their own department before getting the others in on it.

I rang Ernie Bentley at the lab, but he had finally taken off. He had no phone at home and since he'd be back in the loft in the morning, there was no sense bothering him at this hour.

Until now Martrel hadn't questioned me, but I knew what he was thinking. We sat in the semidarkness facing each other and at last he said, "Sonia . . . she is quite safe?"

"I have her downtown. She's waiting there for you."

"That is good. When will we see her?"

"If all goes well, tomorrow."

He nodded. "I have waited a long time."

"Tell me," I said, "why did you make the break? Was it for her?"

He studied me a minute. "I think you know that already, sir."

"Why?"

Martrel looked at his hands, then toward the window. "I am not a young man any longer. My life I have lived for my country and my party. Ah, yes, it was different then when one was young and there was excitement, power and one could manipulate affairs of the world. We all had ideals and foresaw something new. But things change. One gets old.

"I had forgotten that youth can pass you by. Until I met Sonia, women had no part in my life. They were not necessary, at least for me. Those things were replaced by the political aspect we had cultivated and those things became my love. With Sonia . . . ah, well, how can that be said?"

"Easily enough. It happens to everybody."

"Never did I expect it to happen to me. She was so young and lovely . . . so fresh and unspoiled. Suddenly everything changed and I felt young again and all the things that once seemed so important were reduced to nothing. I felt love and saw beauty and at the same time saw that my life had gone into violence and corruption. It was a waste, a sheer waste. All those ideals . . . what had happened to them? Power had destroyed those I knew, the fine world we had visualized was a vile mess now. There was something senseless about it. Sonia had been indoctrinated well through the youth groups, yet I could feel that she had more insight than I had, and it was through my talks with her that she saw it too. I made sure she was able to see the way other people lived and thought, and when she took advantage of an escape route I was happy, very happy indeed. Even though she left me, I was happy. I knew that someday I would follow her."

"You love her?"

"Yes, my friend, I love her. Deeply."

"Suppose she doesn't feel that same way?"

He shook his head and smiled gently. "I know that if I can

see her again ... be with her and speak, that she will love me too."

"Did she?"

"It was something I did not require her to say. She knew well how I felt. It was not necessary for me to say it either."

"When she defected you caught hell."

"It was to be expected. I was suspected, of course, but so not to make it more difficult for her I threw myself even harder into my work. It was not difficult. My experience has been vast, and although there were those in the party who sought my expulsion I had built up a segment who would rather keep me in my position." His smile broadened meaningfully. "As you Americans say, I know where many bodies are buried. It would not have been politically wise to purge me. Later my work satisfied even my staunchest opponents."

He stopped, leaned on the windowsill and looked out over the city at night. Off in the distance you could see the slow stream of traffic going across the George Washington Bridge and the huge signs from the factories on the Jersey side lighting up the night.

I said, "You realize that you're a target, don't you? They want you dead."

"Yes," he told me. "It had to happen."

"If you talk to our people the heat will go off and you can expect protection. Until then you'll stay a target and so will Sonia."

"I have thought about it often." He took a deep breath and sighed. "Even there I have made a few friends."

"Have you?" I asked him softly. "You think they won't turn on you like a snake to protect their own hides? You think the political arrangement is a breeding ground for friendship? Think about it a little more, Martrel."

He pulled back from the window and slumped in his chair. "Yes, you are right, of course. There have been others ... friends ... that defected. I myself saw to their extermination because I considered it necessary. Life itself was not to be measured with political aspiration. Yes, my friend, it is true."

"They're in close now, Martrel. You're running out of time. Eventually they'll backtrack us and the clock will stop. Talk to our people and maybe we can hold things in your favor. Two others are in this country now because they made the big jump. They're safe and they'll stay that way. If we pick your brains they'll have to reorganize their policy and the advantage will move our way. If war is coming it can be put off a few more years at least and maybe by then everything will have changed. You can do it if you want to."

"It will not be easy to break the pattern of a lifetime. I . . . I must see Sonia. Perhaps then . . ."

I didn't want to push him. If he made up his own mind it would come easy, but too much pressure might tumble him the other way too. "Tomorrow," I said. "She's waiting for you."

His face was drawn with fatigue and he looked older than before. I was wondering what he'd do when he found out Sonia's love for him was that of a father for a daughter. If that was enough, it would do. If it wasn't . . . I didn't want to think about it.

I told Martrel to take the bed, and when he stretched out, pulled a couple of chairs together and closed my eyes.

At seven I was up, but Martrel hadn't awakened. He lay there, his breathing heavy, sleeping the sleep of somone totally exhausted. I found coffee, made a pot and scrambled a couple of eggs. At nine I was pacing the room like a restless cat, checked Martrel, saw that he hadn't moved and went downstairs and down the street to the newsstand, picked up a tabloid, threw a nickel in the box and got back to the apartment.

The front-page story was the kidnapping of Gabin Martrel from his room in the hospital and beside a full head shot of him was another of the suspected kidnapper.

Me.

It was a lousy photo, one taken some years ago before I had the scar and there was two days' worth of beard on my face. My hair had been long, and now it was cropped short. Maybe a pro might spot me from the picture, but I doubted if any casual observer would.

The one of Martrel was a beauty though. His face had too many distinguishing features to go unrecognized. But this was New York and it had eight million people in it mostly concerned with their own troubles, and with a little care we might be able to travel without being picked up.

The story was mostly filler, giving Gabin Martrel's history and the details of his defection. Although no leads pointed to his whereabouts, it was thought that his kidnappers were political idealists of the Soviet variety working in conjunction with an American citizen suspected of several crimes, a person for hire to anyone who could buy him.

Brother, they sure tossed that one around. Maybe IATS could bring me out of hiding to deny my guilt and get the

At seven we came up at the Forty-ninth Street exit in the middle of a crowd, and at the newsstand I glanced at the later editions of the papers. As I expected, something else blazed across the front of most of them, and I wasn't worried as far as the public was concerned. But there would be sharper eyes covering the city to their best capabilities, and these were the ones we had to be careful of.

I went in the side door of a corner drugstore where the phone booths were, dropped in a dime and dialed Wally Gibbons' number. It rang six times before it was jerked impatiently off the hook. I knew he'd recognize my voice, and if his line was monitored I didn't want to announce myself. I said, "Say, Wally, sorry to have to bother you, but I need that material I lent you on the Watson-Brice construction case. I'll meet you in an hour down where Bing hangs out. See you later."

I hung up before he could answer, but I heard his breath hissing through his teeth. Two years ago in going through the building the Watson-Brice Company was putting up, he had taken a tumble into a trough of lime and I had had to duck out and get him a new outfit. It had been funny then because he was covered in white and had looked like something out of a comedy show and wouldn't go near the street like that. Bing Willis was an old buddy who practically lived in Stanton's Bar on Broadway before he died, so if Wally put two and two together we'd have Martrel out of his white coveralls.

What I was afraid of was the police knowing how he was traveling. Since we didn't get caught in their net and the only clothes in the apartment were the coveralls, they'd get the idea in a hurry. The only trouble was, they'd be picking up every painter, plasterer or worker using the white pullovers and it would take up their time too.

Rather than stay side by side with Martrel, I walked ahead fifty feet and let him follow me. He'd be the first one spotted if it happened and since the police would only give him protection, I had to be free to operate. We went up Broadway, staying in traffic, crossed over when we reached Stanton's and went inside.

Ron, the day bartender, had gone off duty, but he had the envelope I wanted behind the cash register and the night man handed it over to me and took the buck I offered him. He was too busy making drinks to pay any attention to me and with the place filled with the working crowd including laborers from the new projects going up all over the area, neither Martrel nor myself looked out of place.

I went into the back room where the tables were, picked out a corner booth and sat facing the front. When Martrel slid in he was effectively screened from observation unless you were in the booth on the other side. A waiter hobbled over, took our orders for a couple of sandwiches and beer, wrote it down and left.

Fifteen minutes after he placed them in front of us, Wally Gibbons and Rondine came in, went through the bar and back where he knew I'd be. I had seen him mad before, but the look on his face was something new. I waved him over, reached for Rondine's hand, felt myself turn inside out just to look at her and said, "Hello, doll."

It was hard to read her eyes, but not her smile. "Has it been . . . bad?"

"Rough. Sit down. This is Gabin Martrel."

Wally threw the parcel across the table at me, gave me a glance of sheer frustration, then started to grin. "Damn you, Tiger. Damn you anyway."

"Thanks, buddy."

"Don't thank me. Thank her." He waved a thumb toward Rondine. "I was going to make you suffer. I wanted you to sweat like I've been sweating and she talked me out of it."

"They have a stakeout on your place?"

"Yeah, but it wasn't hard to beat. You realize what kind of hell you've been raising?"

"I've been out of touch."

"Then let me fill you in." He looked at Gabin Martrel, then back at me. "Okay to talk?"

"Go ahead."

"After you got out of the hospital, somebody noticed that the cop who was supposed to be on the door was missing. He didn't wake up to explain right away so they closed the place off from very angle."

"I expected that."

"You were lucky," he said; "somebody else wasn't."

"What do you mean?"

"Down in the basement they found three people who couldn't come up with an ID. Nobody at the hospital recognized them although they claimed to be part of the cleaning staff. The police checked out their stuff and came up with a gimmick designed to wipe out half the floor. One of the big floor buffers was a bomb that could take off the corner of the building and they had planned to leave it outside the door of the room Martrel was in. It would have worked, too."

"The papers didn't have anything about it."

"Orders from on top. They didn't want it released. Three reporters were in the building on something else when everything went flying and they got the story, all right. Dave Severn called me to tell me about it."

Martrel pressed his mouth together and said tightly, "They are very desperate now."

Rondine's hand came across the table and laid on top of mine. "Tiger . . . . should you do this alone?"

"I have no choice."

"You still have your life."

It was coming to a head now; I could see it in her eyes. Any time I could get the ultimatum. It would have been now, but she didn't want me thinking about anything else for the moment. She wanted me clean and clear before she would give it to me straight.

"So have a lot of people, baby. If we do it right, they might keep theirs."

"And yours?"

"It's a job, Rondine. You know it as well as I do. I don't back off an assignment."

When she took her hand away her eyes were sad. I gave the package to Martrel. "Go in the men's room and change. Dump those coveralls in the trash can under the paper towels."

I let him slide out, made sure nobody followed him into the toilet and turned back to Wally. "Let's have the picture on the stakeout."

"Quit worrying. We weren't followed. My building connects

with the one next to it, and we went through the tunnel and
out the back exit of the other one. We caught a cab on the
avenue and came straight here."

"Your line bugged?"

"Damn right. Or else there's fuzz in the transmission."

"It's bugged then."

Wally said, "Look, Bing was pretty well known. Plenty of
people knew about him and this place. If they ran it
through . . ."

"We'll blow as soon as Martrel gets back."

"Those T-men were coming back tonight. Probably there
now. I'm going to have to come up with a damn good story
to please them."

"You'll get one, kid. You'll be right on top of the biggest
you ever saw. I'll need a couple of witnesses to this and you
and Rondine can be them. Mind, doll?"

She smiled, shook her head. "No. Not this time."

I gave Wally the address of the warehouse and the knock
signal that would identify them to Sonia. They were to stay
there with her until Martrel and I showed up and we could get
everything down in black and white our people wanted so
badly. Sonia was to be told to play along with Martrel and
not drop any disappointments down his throat before we were
finished for her safety and his too. The only thing that would
keep them alive was his speaking up. The Soviets had the
pressure on now. They'd have a big team in on this and
operating fast. If we could uncover and knock off their source
of communication we could stop them, but that would have to
wait. The primary thing was protecting Martrel.

I let Rondine and Wally leave, sat there until Martrel came
out in one of Wally's old suits, picked up the check and went
back through the bar and paid the bill.

Once more the rain had started, a soft, warm rain that was
enough to empty the streets and send people running for the
cabs. I didn't like standing there on the corner and told
Martrel to stay with me and start walking for a cross street
where it would be easier to get a ride.

Like the rest of the sidewalk traffic, we stayed close to the
buildings out of the wet, dodging around people coming the
other way. At the first cross street too many people were
waiting for cabs, so we crossed over and continued straight
ahead. At least the rain gave us an excuse to keep our heads
down.

But not far enough. A hand reached out, grabbed my sleeve and a voice said, "Hey . . . hey, mister."

He'd never know how close he came to getting himself killed. My hand was on the .45 and it was halfway out before I recognized the starter from the Tomlinson Building.

"You never gave me my keys back, mister. Boy, I can get in trouble if they find out that set's gone. Look . . ."

I pushed him into the opening of a novelty store with Martrel watching nervously. "Sorry, feller, I was in a hurry." I dug in my pocket and came up with the two keys. My fingers had something else, the photo of Spaad Helo that Ernie had given me.

When the starter took the keys, he said, "That's one of the guys makes deliveries to Fountain's."

I tried to keep my voice quiet. "Oh?"

"Sure. He goes in and out of there regular. Mean-looking guy, that's why I noticed him. Who is he?"

"Nobody important."

"Glad I seen you to get those keys back. Lousy night, ain't it?"

"Not so bad," I said.

He chuckled, dropped the keys in his pocket, turned up his collar and started out into the rain. I looked at Martrel.

His face was a chalk white.

"Can I see that picture, please?"

I handed it to him. "Recognize the guy?"

"Spaad Helo. Yes, I know him very well."

"He's here to kill you, Martrel."

He handed the picture back and looked at me long and hard. "No, I am not his primary assignment."

I felt my hands knot into hard fists. "Spill it."

"He is here on the *Valchek Project*."

And there is was again!

"More. Fast."

"There is a certain building in Washington that contains records and information on Soviet affairs including something new your own people aren't aware of yet. Soon they will get around to deciphering what they have and the Soviet Government will suffer a tremendous setback."

"You know what it is?"

"No, it was handled by another department. I know only of its value. The entire building will be destroyed. That is the *Valchek Project*."

It came to me slowly, accelerating as I found the bits and

pieces and strung them out in a line. It started accidentally and ended deliberately and it wasn't over yet. It could still be too late.

"Martrel . . . look. You're going to have to be on your own."

His eyes were determined now. He had almost made his decision. "Whatever you say."

I gave him the address of the warehouse to memorize, the signal and told him to get there by cab and stay put until I arrived. Wally and Rondine would both be there with Sonia and they would be safe. Nobody else was to be admitted except me and he could give Wally a rundown of the *Valcheck Project* while he waited. If Wally came up with a double-barreled job he'd be in clover with his paper.

This time we walked west until a cab cruised by; I flagged it down in the middle of the street and put Martrel on board. Ten minutes later I got one for myself and had the cabbie drive down to the dock area where the *Maitland* had been berthed, hoping it was still tied up.

The luck of the Irish was still following me around. The dock was lit up with floodlights and there was a lot of activity on the deck. The *Maitland* was getting ready to shove off and there wasn't much time. A five got me use of the dock watchman's phone and I called Charlie Corbinet.

He started to say something, but I cut him off. I told him where I was and to get there as fast as he could. I wanted an IATS team alerted and standing by for some fast action and all their intercom lines cleared. He didn't waste time with questions. Those could come later. He knew I had something and hung up before I did.

The watchman said the ship would be sailing in forty-five minutes, and I checked my watch. I waited outside the gate, looking for cabs coming my way, getting edgier with each passing minute. It took thirty minutes for Charlie to reach me, and I had him hold the cab.

"This better be good, Tiger," was the first thing he said.

"Hold that ship, Charlie. Can you do it?"

"I think so."

Whatever he showed the watchman in his wallet made the guy sputter a little and open the gate for us. We ran down the dock, took the gangplank up to the deck where a big guy stood barring the way with an ugly frown on his scarred and battered face. "What the hell do you guys want?"

"The captain," Charlie said. He flashed the wallet again.

"Damn it, mister, this ship is shoving off. We haven't got time . . ."

"Do what you're told," Charlie said in a cold, stiff voice.

The guy growled, walked off and came back in a minute with a short, bowlegged guy in a weathered blue uniform, looking sore as a teased bull. But he knew authority when he saw it and didn't want to aggravate anything that would keep him from sailing.

"Yes, gentlemen?"

Charlie looked at me. "Your ball, Tiger."

I took out the picture of Spaad Helo and the one of the dead guy he had shot accidentally and held them in the light. "Recognize these two?"

He picked them out of my fingers, studied them carefully and said, "Yes. They came on board when we arrived. Treasury men. I believe they were looking for narcotics. Needless to say, they didn't find any." He tapped the one photo. "This fellow looks dead."

"He is," I said.

"Then what can I do for you?"

"You unloaded a shipment of cases carrying Keipleitz presses and accessories due for delivery in Washington, D.C. What became of them?"

"You'll have to go through another office for that information. The longshoremen, the trucking company, the . . ."

"We haven't got time," I said impatiently. "Everything is closed."

"I'm sorry, I can't help you any further." He handed the pictures back. "Now, if I can get about the business of running a ship . . ."

"Go ahead."

We walked back to the dock and stood there in the floodlights. Charlie said, "Let's have it, Tiger."

"The *Valchek Project.*"

"Damn!" He muttered explosively.

I told him what Martrel had told me about the details of it.

"The Soviets found a way to get inside those buildings. They learned about the presses being delivered there and gimmicked it with a small nuclear bomb. Sometime during the assembly of those presses in the building that thing will go off and wipe out an area as big as a city block."

"How did you come up with this?"

"From a crazy little guy who thought he wasted eighteen

hundred bucks on a Geiger counter. Well, I'd like to tell him it
wasn't exactly wasted, only he's dead now. He was playing
around with that thing and found the device in one of the cases
and called me because he didn't know of anything else to do. I
thought the counter was reacting to one of the luminous dials
on the press and told him about it. I told him about the
screwing he took on the price too. He got pretty drunk up
after it.

"When the *Maitland* came in, the Soviet team on the *Valchek Project* came aboard with forged Treasury Department
identification and made like they were checking for narcotics.
It wasn't too unusual, so nobody suspected anything wrong.
What they really were doing was checking on their cargo.
During that time one of Fletcher's buddies must have told
them about him using the counter around the cargo and that
really got to them. They lifted his gimmick, found him tanked
up and dropped him in the river. He was a little guy who'd
never be missed and they were almost right. The one mistake
was in that guy forgetting to dump the forged Treasury Department ID. Wally Gibbons called and found out no T-men
were ever on the *Maitland* this trip and the whole bit just
came to me. All this time I was writing it off as being part of
their usual closed-mouthed way of operating."

"We can make it in time. We'll open up every office concerned with that shipment if we have to. Come on."

"Where to?"

"All the IATS wheels are gathered to hear your story, and
they want it firsthand. It's the only chance you have of getting
off the hook."

"Maybe."

"It's better than nothing."

And they were waiting. The way vultures wait for a body to
die before they feast on it. A dozen of them sat along each
side of a long mahogany table looking at me, some with frozen
animosity, others with near curiosity, watching the man they
had heard so much about. Hal Randolph was at the far end,
and four stenographers stood by, taking down a verbatim
report.

It was Charlie's play and he wasted no time on it. He was
the Colonel of old who knew what to do and how to do it
and would tolerate no interference. He was part of them, yet
still part of me and regardless of either it was national security
he was after and going to get. It was war and we had to win.

I spun it out in detail while they listened, deliberately omitting the Martrel affair, and showed them the *Valchek Project* the way it happened. Later they'd get to Martrel, but not yet, not just yet.

I had hardly finished before one of those who had been the curious type had a phone in his hand and was issuing orders. Whoever he was, he pulled a lot of weight because Hal Randolph jumped at his word and got on another phone to pull out the stops. They were going into the files of the shipping company, locating the delivery trucks and the present whereabouts of the cases. They weren't taking any chances on me being wrong with a deal like this and with all the time the presses had had, delivery could already have been effected and assembly begun.

Suddenly, Hal Randolph held up his hand for quiet. "Washington on the line," he said. There was a hush across the room and everybody watched him carefully. His face seemed to get ashen and he said, "Those presses arrived this morning. They're in the basement of the R-1 building and undergoing assembly."

The other man with him said, "Stop them. Clear the area and get a team down there immediately." He found one of the other phones, called the operator and told her to get an Air Force chopper to stand by for an immediate pickup, then assembled his group to leave. Only three of them and Randolph stayed behind.

He walked over to me, his eyes no longer curious. "This will go in your favor, of course, but you have more to answer for. Right now you are under arrest."

"Thanks a bunch," I said.

When they left, Randolph came up with the others, smiling at me through a thin, hard mouth. "I've been waiting for this, Mann. I'm going to watch you squirm from now on. Your goddamn antics have cost me plenty and I'm just the guy who likes a little repayment in kind."

I grinned back at him. "Maybe I can spread a little of the honey your way too."

The grin stayed, but it hurt. "What's that supposed to mean?" he asked.

"So you took a few lumps on my account. Maybe you need a little prize of your own to put you back in good standing again."

"I can do without any favors."

"But the country can't, buddy," I said. I wasn't grinning at all now. "Let's not get involved with any personal garbage until the big picture's cleared. This thing isn't over yet."

He looked at me, waiting. So did the others. Charlie's eyes were narrow slits and he was enjoying the moment as much as I was, content to let me do it my way.

"I think I know how we can break their communication down. I know where the cell is operating out of."

One of the men said something under his breath. Randolph's face started to get red and his teeth were a white slash in his face. "We're not making any deals, Tiger."

"Then go to hell," I said quietly.

His hand reached for my lapel and almost made it. I grabbed his wrist and pushed it away. "Lay off."

"You can be made to talk."

"I have a lot of scars from people who thought the same thing but I haven't done it yet. Unless you've refined a lot of techniques you're going to have a hard time doing it."

Charlie pushed in between us. "Say what you want to say, Tiger."

I nodded and smiled at Randolph. "Like a ten-minute start into the street."

"Sure," he said coldly.

"You're committing yourself too easily, friend. I want it confirmed."

"If you think . . ."

Charlie said, "I know this man, Hal. He won't talk unless you agree. If you do, I want that agreement kept."

Randolph looked like he would burst. "How stupid do you think I am?"

"Pretty stupid if you don't come through fast," Charlie interrupted. "We have to make deals all the time anyway. This isn't anything unusual. I'll vouch for this man's character and integrity right down the line and if you think you're hurting now from departmental pressure, just let him be right and that cell gets a chance to pull out and then, my friend, you'll really see pressure. You'll get it from me, from Washington, from Martin Grady, from the papers and anything else I can bring to bear. You'll hold down a paper clip job the rest of your life."

I had to laugh. I didn't think the Colonel still had that tone of voice in him. Randolph knew he meant every word he said and he stood there wishing me dead and not being able to make it happen. It took a minute for him to cool down, stalking about the room in a frenzy, but he finally came back and said, "Okay, Mann . . . you bought it. Where do we go from here?"

"The Tomlinson Building on Broadway," I told him.

The guard at the desk at the end of the hall sat hunched over a newspaper and waved unconcernedly when we asked to check the night book. Only a few people had signed in, none on the floor we wanted. The elevator was on automatic and three of us got in, Charlie, Randolph and me, while the others took the stairs up to cover them.

When we reached the floor, we waited for the others, posted two men by the elevators and one at the stairs while we went down to the door. At first it looked like it was dark inside, then I saw a tiny seepage of light from the bottom corner of the door. I whispered to Charlie, "The glass is painted black and there's a felt liner at the bottom." He looked at the thin streak of light and nodded. "Somebody's in there," I said.

Charlie moved us off quietly to one side. "We'll have to hit it quick."

"Let's take the glass. I'll bust it with a fire ax and you can cover anybody inside with your guns. It's a simple layout, just one big room and you can stop the action from the doorway."

I opened the case on the wall, pulled out the red-handled ax and hefted it, then walked back to the door. Charlie and Randolph stood to one side to give me room to swing, black police positives ready in their hands. When they were ready, I held the ax sideways to wipe out as much of the pane with one swing as I could and brought the ax around in an arc.

The glass shattered and spilled into the room with a crash that echoed down the halls, the light from the room bathing us with unshaded brilliance but too much of the glass was still there and I had to chop at it again. The funny little guy in the black suit who had jumped up from the desk with fear distorting his face let out an unintelligible curse and dove to one side under the table.

Randolph almost reached inside to find the locks on the door, and I gave him a shove just in time. A gun blasted and a bullet thudded against the doorjamb where he had been a second before. Charlie threw a couple of fast ones in the general direction of the gunshot but I knew he wasn't hitting anything.

Two more slugs pounded through the door from the inside and I heard the guy scramble someplace else again. I waved them back, stayed with the wall as protection and started tearing away with the ax, chopping at the door around the locks.

I almost had it through when one of the bullets smashed into the handle as I landed and the wood splintered and the head flew inside the room and skittered across the room. The men at the stairs didn't move until Randolph called to them, but we needed concerted firepower now and if we could spray the room from all angles we had a chance of nailing him. But he had a better chance of nailing us.

Randolph had everybody in place, the angles set, when we all looked at each other simultaneously. There was the gentle odor of smoke coming out the door. Randolph said, "Damn, he's burning papers. We'll have to rush him."

"And get how many killed?" Charlie mused.

I lifted the .45 in my hand, aimed it into the room at the sprinkler head set in the ceiling, squeezed the trigger and felt the gun buck in my hand. The sprinkler head flew into pieces and water poured out of the pipes. It wasn't a directed stream, but apparently it was effective enough. There was a curse and another pair of shots poked holes in the bottom part of the door.

Then Randolph gave the signal to fire and while the automatic fire alarm sounded a discordant bonging throughout the building, the staccato bark of six guns blazing away built up an unearthly symphony of death.

He screamed from inside but they didn't stop the shooting. Each gun reloaded and again and in the middle of it the scream sounded again and choked off into a rattling cough.

We couldn't wait any longer. We hit that door repeatedly until it came off the hinges and the locks at the same time and slammed to the floor and we went in over the debris ready to

fire at the first sign of movement. But we didn't have to worry
about that. The guy lay crumpled up where he fell, blood
oozing from two holes in his stomach, a rasping moan coming
through the pink froth of his lips.

One of the men stamped out the sheets of paper that were
still smoking, protected by the desk, while another clamped his
hand over the waterpipe to keep the cascade off our necks.
Coming down Broadway below us was the flashing red of the
fire trucks answering the alarm that went off when I blew the
sprinkler, filling the air with the raucous sound of their hooters.

I stood by them while they gathered the papers and laid
them out on the desk. Charlie said, "What do they mean,
Tiger?"

It was part of the pad that looked like nothing more than a
cheap way of recording special orders. I said, "This is their
channel of communication. My guess is that the guy on the
floor is Fountain."

One of the men bending over him held up a wallet.
"That's what his driver's license says. Nothing else here
though."

"Will he make it?"

The man shook his head at Charlie. "Unconscious now.
He's had it."

I flipped the sheets over, trying to make something of it.
"Whenever he needed someone he worked it through his
advertisements. It's probably all coded but it shouldn't be too
hard to break. If he was this interested in burning this pad it
must mean something." I rummaged through the desk and
brought out the sheaf of special orders I had seen before and
handed them over. "These might tie in too. Most of the
business was legitimate enough and a good cover for the
operation If he headed it up, we might be able to break
through the code and nail the agents. That is, if these names
mean that."

Randolph had stopped being hostile. He took the pages
and the orders from my hand. "You hit it, Mann. These
special orders and their replies are probably coded instructions.
I'll get these downtown and get our people on it. It won't take
long to get the answers."

Over by the table one of the IATS men called, "The guy's
coming around."

I went over with Randolph and Charlie and knelt down
beside him. Nobody interfered or objected. The guy glared up

at me with hate-filled eyes close to death. "Spaad," I said. "Spaad Helo."

Even then he tried to sneer. "We'll bury you," he barely croaked.

"But you first, buddy." I took out the .45, thumbed the hammer back and held it against his belly below the other two wounds. "This one won't kill you any faster, but it will sure make it hurt worse. I want Spaad Helo."

Something changed in his eyes. He looked up at the others, then me.

I said, "I'm not one of them. Maybe you know me. Tiger Mann is my name."

His nod was barely perceptible.

"Spaad Helo," I reminded him. "Where is he? Or do you want another slug?"

He was going to talk. He wanted to talk in the worst way. His face was wild with pain and the thought of more was too much for him. He opened his mouth to speak and the effort was too much. His head fell back limply and he was dead.

I stood up and put the .45 back. Randolph was looking at me with a strange expression. "Would you have done it, Tiger?"

"Certainly. Why not?"

He made a peculiar face and turned away. Outside in the hall, feet were pounding on the floor and shouts rang throughout the building. Charlie said, "You better go tell them, Hal. We'll get things together here."

I found some cartons and we started loading everything in the room. The firemen came in, still not liking Randolph's explanation, but being able to do nothing about it. One of them stopped the flow of water temporarily, and we stacked everything on the table into the boxes.

At the far end of the room was a closet that took up the entire wall space and when one of Randolph's men opened it he dragged out boxes of stockings, cheap, frilly underwear, kitchen gadgets and all the other junk Fountain had dealt in. "What about this stuff?"

Charlie looked at it, said, "Leave this until later. We'll check everything out, but right now the paperwork is the important thing."

I nodded agreement, but didn't feel right. Something else was there in my mind, another needle trying to prick into my conscious thoughts. I stopped, prowled around the room through the litter of junk, looking over the stuff they were stacking into the cartons, and couldn't put my finger on it. I went back to the desk, scoured it for anything at all, but by then everything was gone from it.

The first cop that came in the room saw me there and had a gun in his hand before anybody could stop him. "Hold it, you."

Charlie caught the action and nudged Randolph.

I waited. The cop came up and said, "Turn around."

Before he asked me, I took the position up against the wall, leaning there with feet back and spread, let the cop pull the .45 from the rig and pat me down.

I heard Charlie say, "Well?"

Randolph laughed. "I said *I'd* give him a ten-minute start, but it's out of my hands now."

Until then I never realized how cutting old Charlie could be. "You're in it now, Hal. Maybe your wife would like to know about that episode in Detroit."

The guy almost choked. "You wouldn't!"

"In the pig's ass I wouldn't."

Hal Randolph said something I couldn't catch, walked over and shoved his wallet under the cop's nose. "I'll take care of him."

The cop didn't budge. "Sorry, mister. We have him on the wanted sheet."

"You better check my authority," he said.

"I saw it. Maybe it will impress the captain, but not me." The cop tapped my waist. "Straighten up with your hands behind you." I heard the rattle of handcuffs as he took them from his leather case.

Randolph said, "Then you'd better check this before you ride departmental charges." Whatever he showed the cop changed his mind in a hurry. I turned around and the two of them were facing each other down and the cop had lost the issue. I held out my hand for the gun and he put it back, his face seething with anger. Abruptly, he spun on his heel and walked out of the room.

"Thanks," I told him. "You had me worried. Someday I'm going to find out what happened in Detroit too."

The hard look came back again and I knew I had stepped over the boundary line. Randolph looked at his watch with an elaborate gesture. "You got ten minutes, Tiger, then we go on you again. I'll pull every string I know and close off every avenue of escape and when I have you on the boards we'll settle you, Martin Grady and his whole damn organization at once. You can't get far in ten minutes. You can't beat a radio or a phone, so the second you leave here start thinking what it cost you to be a wise guy."

"You aren't the grateful type," I said.

"Mann, you're wasting your own valuable time."

"I can still get off the hook, Randolph."

"No, you can't."

"Mister," I said, "you have a short memory. You still haven't got Martrel and you still haven't got his statement. You still haven't found Spaad Helo and if I come up with that kind of kicker I'll make you and your agency a trade that will cream you. I'll get off the hook all the way down the line with some left over and you'll be sucking eggs for being snotty. I delivered you a bundle of goodies that ought to put you up for a medal or a promotion, which is what you couldn't do for yourself. If you think I have to stop there, you're nuts."

"You have eight minutes left."

"Stuff 'em up your tail."

He grinned, pleased with himself, liking the way I was mad. You forget things when you're boiling over and that's what he wanted. But then I saw Charlie's warning look, kissed them all off with one glance and got out of there.

Just before the elevator hit the lobby level I remembered something and touched the stop button at the first floor. I got out, took the stairs down, flattened against the wall and took a look out into the corridor. The cop from upstairs was there with a few others, one in a captain's uniform, and the brass was chewing out the patrolman for giving in to the Washington type no matter who he was. He told one to stay at the elevators, another to guard the stairwell and then climbed in the other elevator with the uniformed cop.

Before the patrolman reached me, I circled down the staircase to the basement level, found an exit door that opened in the rear of the building and went through it. I had to scramble over two fences before I found a way out to the cross street and made the sidewalk without being spotted by anyone. Those cops never forgave anyone who slugged one of their kind.

I shoved my hands in my pockets against the rain and walked toward Eighth Avenue.

What was missing? What did I know that pointed a finger at something that was there but I couldn't see? From now on it was all so simple. A detailed statement from Martrel and everybody would be happy. He was with the broad he was in love with, and knowing she was safe was all he wanted.

He was luckier than me in a way. He was old enough to realize Sonia wasn't for him, and age can have its benefits. But who could tell? Maybe she was for him after all. Maybe the father image was what she needed. There were other similar arrangements that had worked out fine.

Not with Rondine, though. My business was something she could never understand and didn't want to hear about. To her it was a past that was over and done with. She couldn't live with the fear and the danger and I couldn't blame her a bit. It wasn't a woman's way of living.

How the hell do you cut twenty years out of your life? How do you stop something so ingrained as the thing in me? How could I tell her that we'd never really be safe no matter where we were or what we called ourselves? There would always be a Spaad Helo somewhere, always an assignment to bring home my head because they couldn't take a chance on me not being out of the action. I knew as much about them as they did about me and it was safer with me dead than alive.

How many of us were left now? I thought. Only a handful from the original bunch. Not many at all. Only the lucky ones. Or the good ones. The law of averages had caught up with most of them. And Rondine and Charlie would be right. The organization would go on. Martin Grady's work would contin- ue, supplementing the governmental agencies in a way they couldn't do themselves. Others would train, take the field and pile up the experience until they were as good as the best. In a little while I wouldn't even be missed. Thought of fondly when the old group got together, but not missed. If I got killed or cut out I'd never be missed.

Patriots? One of the IATS boys had called us traitors once. Balls. They didn't like us infringing on their activities. They discarded the fact that we were all trained pros, but of a little different caliber. We were a hard bunch too, fighting on a frontier as wild and as new as anything that ever existed in the old West. We had died with the best of them, backing up their plays and sometimes leading the field. They never beefed when they needed an extra gun or information only Martin Grady's money could buy.

Rondine wouldn't accept the excuse though. Even if it hurt it would be the big good-bye for both of us, and like the man said, thanks for the memories. What would I replace them with? Thoughts of other women? Some of them had been pretty nice. Sweet-smelling from a bath, perfumed, some gamey and wild with the aroma of fresh hay in their hair, and low, chuckling laughter. Some in excitingly brief pieces of silk or nylon, some in gowns that swirled and billowed as they danced. Some . . .

I stopped dead in the street, said, *"Damn it all to hell!"* in a hoarse whisper and felt the sweat start to ooze out of the pores on the back of my neck. My hands shook as I looked at my watch. It was almost five-thirty in the morning, and I had run through time as though it had no meaning at all.

And then, suddenly, I knew where Spaad Helo would be. I knew what all the answers were and where the big finger pointed. I sprinted to a diner on the corner, found the coin box and dropped in a dime to dial Charlie Corbinet's number. It rang and rang but there was no answer and I hung up. I stepped out of the booth, trying to decide what to do. I could call the cops, but they'd be quicker to pick me up than to listen to what I had to say. If they did and made a wrong move, a lot of people would die.

Dimly, the radio the counterman had turned on was blaring out the news on the half hour. The announcer was talking calmly but couldn't keep the excitement out of his voice. One of our secret agencies had just stopped the possible destruction of a major government building in Washington, and although the investigation was top secret, he felt more information would be forthcoming by the next broadcast.

So they did it. They got there in time. But was it enough?

I flagged a cab down, gave him the address of the warehouse and told him to let me off on the corner. He nodded, hit the flag and cut down to the West Side Highway to take the easy way downtown.

When we were up on the ramp, I could look over the whole city and see it for what it was. Of all the hours, these were the only moments the city, the concrete and steel Gargantua, took time off to sleep. In the east was the first gray of the false dawn, and with it the rain eased off to a mist that stopped before we got to the turnoff.

Whether Randolph or the other liked it or not, I knew there'd be a bulletin out on me and every patrol car would be in on the search, every beat cop alerted. It was so damn deserted here that any moving thing would come under suspicion and I couldn't afford getting stopped now.

I whipped off the raincoat, afraid the light tan would be too visible, and tossed it in an ash can on the sidewalk. In the black suit I wore deliberately I wouldn't be too noticeable. Besides myself, nothing moved along the sidewalks. Once in a while a car would come down from the ramp, then take the cross street and disappear.

Twice a slow-moving prowl car drifted by and I stepped back into the shadows, working my way toward the row of buildings. When I came to the end one, I cut around behind it, found the steel ladder that led to the roof and went up to the top and crouched there in the darkness, looking for anyone who might be waiting.

In the east the sky was getting lighter. Another half hour and the sun would come up. Another sunrise.

How many had died this time? How many more would die before the sun started its travel downward in the west? Who wouldn't live to see the new day ... and if the wrong ones died, how many other lives would pay for it?

I got ready, crawled across the rooftop toward a chimney, held a second before moving on to the parapet on the other side, then clambered over it to drop on the next roof. My rubber-soled shoes didn't make much of a sound, but the small crunch of gravel there sounded like minor explosions. It was all clear there too but I had to be sure. When I was, I edged to the back, went over the last brick and tile separation and let myself down slowly.

I knew where I was. I had used this building before and checked every inch of the layout. It had been renovated for our benefit by Martin Grady for any such eventuality, and, unless it had been given a careful going-over, they wouldn't know about the old skylight that led into the room below.

But they wouldn't be expecting me that way. They'd be expecting a signal knock on the door like I said I'd give and would be waiting. The odds were still going for me if I played it right. My fingers found the skylight, lifted it on well-oiled hinges and propped it there, then I swung over, got my feet on the rungs of the ladder, lowered the skylight over my head and went down the ladder to the top floor.

The staircase was quiet, constructed of steel latticework. I got the handrail under my fingers, the .45 in my other hand and cocked the hammer back. When I felt the concrete under my feet I knew the door was directly ahead and held out my hand to feel for the latch.

Inside I could hear the muted murmur of voices.

Familiar voices.

It had to be quick. This passage was designed as an exit

way, not an entry. From the other side they'd never know the door was there, because it was backed up with planking that looked like the rest of the wall. I'd have seconds working for me but no longer and if I couldn't do the job then it would never be done at all. I had to go through, spot the right one and do it quick.

No second chances.

The other one would be as fast as I was and if he wasn't in position where I could see him he could grab the edge.

Well, there was only one way to find out. I squeezed the latch, knew when it was ready. Then I put my shoulder against the door and shoved it wide open and went in with a crazy scream pulling at my throat like some animal.

In the fraction of a second I saw them, Rondine and Martrel trussed up on the floor and the big guy in the overcoat near the other door wheeling around to see me with eyes tightened into slits, the gun in his hand going off even before it got all the way on me.

My own .45 was bucking in my hand and I saw the shots slam into his body and smash him against the wall as the roar and smoke of two weapons filled the room with deafening echos. Even with the massive tonnage of the .45's in him he didn't die. He tried to mouth a curse and lift the rod only this time it was pointed at Martrel and my next shot kicked it out of his hand and the one following punctuated his forehead with a hole right in the middle and Spaad Helo died with his hat full of his own brains in a heap on the floor.

Her screaming didn't get through to me, but her eyes did. Rondine's had living terror in them and before I read them right it was too late. A slug from the blast of gunfire coming out of the front part of the building tore into my upper arm and the gun dropped out of my hand. I dropped and rolled and felt another slug crease my cheekbone. I tried to grab for the .45 with my left hand. A deliberately aimed shot skittered it away, and the bullet ricocheted up into the ceiling.

My luck had run out.

"If you move I'll kill the girl," Sonia said.

Martrel let out a small cry of despair. He looked years older now, completely defeated.

I sat up, my hand over the bullet hole in my arm. I pulled out a handkerchief and put a tourniquet around the wound, holding it tight with my fingers.

"We have been waiting for you," Sonia told me as she walked into the room.

"I know."

"We should have searched the place more thoroughly. Perhaps then Spaad would not have died. It is what happens when one gets careless." She looked at the huddled form by the wall, not at all touched by the sight. "You have been careless too, my Tiger."

"It happens."

"Had there been others with you, they would have been here by now. I think I can safely assume you are alone, no?"

"More will come later." There was no sense trying to lie to her. She knew the score as well as I did.

"By then you shall be dead. I will not worry. You were much too concerned not to reveal where you hid me. I will tell them that I was in another place."

"Good for you."

I looked at Rondine lying there on her side, feet together, hands tied behind her back the same way Martrel was.

I said, "Sorry, doll. I didn't want it to be this way."

There was an unbelievable coolness in her voice. It was the way the English must have been when Hitler was dropping buzz bombs down their throats. "It's all right, darling."

"How touching."

Rondine looked at her and Sonia seemed to tighten up. It was the peasant being stared down by the grand lady of the castle and even though Sonia was in the commanding position there was something in the difference between the species that was frightening. Her once-soft lips tightened and there was a new coarseness in her high-cheekboned face. Her mouth twisted in a sneer and she said to Rondine, "You can never win."

Deliberately, Rondine smiled at her, said, "We can never lose."

I thought for a moment she was going to pull the trigger on the flat little automatic, but she didn't. Martrel twisted on the floor, his voice trembling. "Sonia . . . please."

"Traitor!" she spit at him. "Filthy swine. Do you think you would live to betray us? Did you think I was like you? No, never. I did not defect, old man. I was sent here. I was ordered to do what I did and hold myself in readiness and that I did. I was here to prepare myself to kill someone like you if we needed it. Now that time has come."

I grimaced, let the tourniquet loosen, then tightened it again. "Your group is gone, Sonia. You're the last one left and you're wide open. We busted your communications at

Fountain's, squashed the *Valchek Project* and got a line on all the agents Fountain had listed. Pretty soon they'll decode your name on his list and you're going to be hunted down like a damn mad dog. Every one of you."

It stopped her. She turned back to me, her eyes blazing. "You did it then!"

"That's right, honey. Me. The Tiger. I did it."

She had to be sure. She wanted to know and couldn't keep the word from escaping her. "How?"

I took my time about it. Time was the only thing I had left. With time I could think of something. Maybe.

I said, "Your pretty little exotic bikini underwear, chicken. It gave you away. Your communications with Fountain were always covered in order blanks and to keep up the pretense with the return instructions he sent you went items of merchandise. Oh, nothing special, nothing any dame with taste would wear, but cheap crap he fed the suckers all over the country.

"But you had a thing with you. Background, upbringing, whatever you call it. I call it no class. Your taste was lousy and you couldn't bring yourself to toss the stuff away. You told me yourself . . . in your country the women eat that stuff up. It has a capitalistic feel about it and is frowned upon, but they love it.

"When I saw that junk Fountain had stored away I should have known then, but it took awhile to get through to me. Brother, did I fall into your cute little trap. Here you were assigned to get to Martrel and I went and did it all for you. It was a nice operation, kid, but it wasn't working fast enough so the rest of the team tried other means. They all got nailed too. It's going to be a long time before your people can put a group like that together again."

"They were stupid to get caught."

"So was I."

Sonia Dutko looked at me with amused surprise. I was still playing for time, but still not there with an answer. "Oh?"

"I could have stopped you when your friend over there dressed like a woman to get to you with instructions, and Ann Lighter walked in on you. That note you took from her was signed T. Mann. There was no 'Tiger' on it, yet you called me that on our first contact. Ann never would have revealed that much, but a Commie agent knowing me from their 'A' list would have it. That was your mistake, kid."

She waved the gun in her hand. "But not a fatal one like yours." She glanced at the others. "Or theirs." I saw Martrel's face and watched her smile at him. "The poor fool, now that he knows he would talk his head off. Look how he looks at me. To get even he would reveal everything."

Behind Martrel, Wally moaned, fought against his ropes, gave up and started swearing. I heard my name a dozen times before he stopped. Rondine knew what I was trying to do and added her own thoughts. "Why don't you shoot us now?"

"Because I am going to do even something better with that suitcase Comrade Helo brought here." I followed her eyes to the black bag by one of the chairs. "Do you know what's in there?"

I knew, all right.

To Rondine, Martrel and Wally she said, "An explosive charge, my friends. You will all die together. They will not know who you are or why you died for a long, long time. By then we will have the situation nicely controlled, because you see, my Tiger, you are going to do something for me Gabin was forced to do earlier."

She reached in her pocket and brought out several sheets of folded paper. "To save their lives he signed a statement that he was not here of his own free will, but was taken forcibly and held by agents of your country and believes they will kill him if he does not talk. He swears unswerving loyalty to our glorious Soviet Union, and this, my Tiger, is your downfall. When news of this gets to the United Nations and is properly exploited it will give us great cause for complaint and will be another wedge driven between your country and the undecided ones."

My skin felt cold. Even the pounding in my arm stopped.

"They know I'm not a Commie lover."

"Ah, but they do not know that you are *not* in the employ of this country either. You will sign a statement too and will swear that you were assigned to kidnap and kill Martrel before he could make his true views known to the world." She smiled, her eyes hard. "You *did* this very well too. You *did* kidnap him and he will be found dead. With the newspapers I think we will have enough to put you in an embarrassing position."

"Suppose I don't sign?"

"But you will." She glanced over to Rondine. "I will shoot her so that it will be very painful. She will not die clean and easy like the rest of you and you will have to watch her suffer before death comes. No, I think you will sign."

As if she were home in her own apartment, Rondine said with no trace of fear or nervousness, "Don't sign it, Tiger."

"You would rather be shot?"

"Others have been shot before me. There will be more too, but we can still retain our sense of loyalty."

"You will not think like that with a bullet in your stomach," Sonia told her, enjoying every word.

"Perhaps not, but if it will keep him from signing that paper I'm quite willing to force your hand."

She meant it, too. Damn if she didn't mean it! But I wasn't going to let her do it. I said, "Shut up, Rondine."

I watched her smile, saw her blow a kiss toward me and caught the fierce look in her eyes. "I'm not your Rondine, remember? Maybe she would rather have died fast and lose what she was dying for. I'm Edith, another person. Although you call me by her name, I'm a different person from her, darling."

"It's no good," I told her.

"Then you did all this for nothing? We all die for no reason. I thought you believed in what you did. I thought you believed in your work. You were so . . . so dedicated. I wanted you to leave it until I realized that you never could and I was ready to live with that too. I knew it had to be done and you had to do it and I was ready to take you and live with it. Now I'm ready to die for your principles, Tiger. I think it's the least you can let me do."

She was all mine then; even trussed up, beaten, she was a winner and all mine and she had bought the time I needed!

For a second I thought it was too late and the gun would go off before I could stop it, but I said, "Sonia . . . hold it. I'll sign the thing."

Her smile was a triumphant thing that she turned on Rondine, a conquering of the lady by the serf. "You are being very wise, my Tiger. I will be sad when you are dead. Only for a very short time because I will remember the sunrises we had together, then I will forget."

Slowly, she backed to the dead body of Spaad Helo on the floor, reached in his pocket and yanked out a pair of thin, hard, steel handcuffs and threw them to me. "Put one on your left wrist and another on the pipe beside you. Tightly. I can see what you do. I know all the devices."

I picked up the cuffs, snapped them on my left arm, my

right hurting like hell with every move I made. Then I shackled myself to the pipe. She came near me, the gun cocked and pointed toward my head. She reached in her pocket, tugged out a pad and threw it at my feet. "I will dictate," she said. "You shall write."

"Please, Tiger," Rondine said softly. Her eyes were wet, tasting the bitterness of defeat.

"Drop it, honey. It's all hers. It had to end sometime."

"Not like this."

I picked up the pad. "Shut up, I said!"

She sobbed once, her breath catching in her throat. I fumbled in my pocket and found Ernie's ball-point pen that had the explosive charge of three sticks of dynamite when it went off, slipped the cap off and stuck it on the other end. "Go ahead," I said.

Sonia gave it to me, three pages' worth of the most incriminating evidence against our country as possible, making me document it to her satisfaction, spelling out the details so each one could be checked and proven if necessary. Briefly, I saw Wally looking at me in open-mouthed horror and the resignation on Martrel's face, the disgust and hatred he had for an old regime that could so completely warp the mind of someone he thought he loved. And the disappointment that was on Rondine's.

I put it all down, signed it with the blood flowing down my arm and sat back feeling all washed out. She waited until I finished, got the suitcase from the wall, opened it and set a timer inside that began to click away with a quiet, ominous sound. "In five minutes it will all be over," she told us. "You may scream and shout if you wish, but there is no one to hear you. This place is well soundproofed and no one will be on the street yet. It is much too early for that. It is just dawn."

I waited until she was ready, gave the top of the pen the necessary twist, stuck the clip over the sheets of paper and held them out to her. She reached for them, took them out of my hand without taking her eyes off my face and stuck them in her pocket. A streak of pain shot through my arm then and it was almost pleasant because the grimace it brought to my face hid what I knew she'd see in my eyes.

"Thank you, my Tiger. I almost regret not being able to see you again. It is good-bye now."

I didn't answer her. I let her go, hearing the ticking of the timer in the suitcase. She kicked the body of Spaad Helo aside, opened the door and went through it, closing it behind her.

Rondine said, *"Oh, Tiger, why did you!"*

Time was the factor again. Seconds of it. The pipe I was shackled to was a blind one that rose ten feet from the floor and was capped off at the top. I almost screamed at the pain that tore through my arm, but I climbed that damn pipe, slid the cuff over the top and dropped to the floor on my hands and knees, then pulled the wires from the charge in the bag.

I untied Wally first and didn't take time for the others. "Drag them to the back. Quick. We have to get a couple of walls between us."

He knew better than to ask questions. He got Martrel under the arms while I tugged at Rondine with my one good arm. We got through the back and out into the yard behind a pile of concrete blocks and as we did the whole world seemed to erupt above us in a shower of flame, smoke and dust.

When it settled I got up, untied Rondine and Martrel, looked into her eyes that were completely knowing now, realizing that I did have an ace and played it and we had won after all. Together we walked around the rubble to the front of the building, hearing the faint shriek of sirens that were coming our way.

We could welcome them now, I thought. I could welcome almost anything.

The sun was just coming up in the east, the crescent tip of it a brilliant orange, reaching out to light the earth with fiery fingertips of a new day.

Sonia was still there with me, but she wasn't watching this sunrise. In essence, she was almost a part of it, a sparkling wet, red splash on the grey rubble of the building that reflected the glow of a fresh day and a job that was all over.

Mysteries You'll Enjoy

WHO KILLED SWEET SUE?   **by Henry Kane**
Blackmail, murder, and a gorgeous trouble-making red-head challenge the intrepid Peter Chambers.
(#D2575—50¢)

TOO FRENCH AND TOO DEADLY   **by Henry Kane**
Hard-living private-eye Peter Chambers plays tag with a killer as he investigates a baffling suicide.
(#G2520—40¢)

THE MANCHURIAN CANDIDATE   **by Richard Condon**
A Korean War hero is brain-washed and becomes an assassin against his will.   (#T1826—75¢)

**INSPECTOR MAIGRET AND THE STRANGLED STRIP-
PER**   **by Georges Simenon**
The famous Inspector Maigret in the Paris underworld of prostitutes, addicts, and killers. Two additional Maig-ret mysteries are published in Signet editions, along with Simenon's recent bestseller, *The Bells of Bicêtre*.
(#D2580—50¢)

THE BODY IN THE BED   **by Bill S. Ballinger**
A hardboiled mystery of the Chicago underworld and a criminal tangle of greed and deceit that erupted into a triple murder.   (#G2569—40¢)

BULLETS ARE MY BUSINESS   **by John B. West**
Private-eye Rocky Steele copes with gunman, a bevy of blondes, and the murder of a beautiful woman.
(#D2571—50¢)

THE HIGH WIRE   **by William Haggard**
This sophisticated spy-thriller comes to a hair-raising cli-max as the protagonist faces his enemy in a cable car stranded high above the Alps.   (#D2519—50¢)

AN EYE FOR AN EYE   **by John B. West**
Murder in Manhattan—the victim—a beautiful blonde heiress.   (#G2567—40¢)

CALL FOR THE DEAD by John Le Carré

A canny British secret agent copes with an unusual case of espionage and murder. By the author of the superlative bestseller, *The Spy Who Came in from the Cold*.

(#D2495—50¢)

DEATH LIKES IT HOT by Edgar Box

The Social Register set, week-ending in East Hampton, plays host to a cut-throat killer. (#G2540—40¢)

DEATH BEFORE BEDTIME by Edgar Box

A senator is murdered in this sizzling close-up of Washington society. (#G2550—40¢)

THE VENETIAN BLIND by William Haggard

Set in London, Venice, and Dusseldorf, a stunning tale of intrigue by a new British master of the spy-thriller.

(#D2393—50¢)

TROT by David Ely

An Army CID investigator gets caught up in a corrupt racket in the Paris underworld. (#D2447—50¢)

INSPECTOR MAIGRET IN NEW YORK'S UNDER-WORLD by Georges Simenon

Breathless pursuit from plush Fifth Avenue to the slums of the Bronx. By the author of the new bestseller, *The Bells of Bicêtre*. (#D2578—50¢)

NERVE by Dick Francis

Unexplained suicides among the jockeys baffle the steeple-chase set in this thunderingly vital suspense novel.

(#P2607—60¢)

MY BUSINESS IS MURDER by Henry Kane

Two exciting mysteries in one book featuring that invincibly tough investigator, Peter Chambers.

(#D2547—50¢)